Tent Rocks

A Novel

M. A. Estevis

Tent Rocks

First Edition

All Rights Reserved

©2018 M. A. Estevis

ISBN 9780692134597

Omni-Media Publishing
Edinburg, Texas

Tent Rocks

A Novel

M. A. Estevis

Other Books by This Author

Down Garrapata Road

Chicken Foot Farm

Goat Creek Crossing

Welcome to Tecolote, Texas

Dudley's Daughter

Prologue

A man in a black suit and a wide-brimmed hat walked silently down a hospital corridor. He hesitated at an open doorway, flashed a badge to an armed guard seated nearby, and entered the dimly-lit room.

Stopping at the foot of the hospital bed, he looked down at a small, wizened man. "I got here as soon as I could. What's going on, Flaco?"

The man in the bed slowly opened his eyes. "Is that you, *carnal*? I wondered if you got my message."

"Uh-huh. I got it last night. But what's happened?" The man in the black suit moved around to the side of the bed.

The small man grimaced. "El Tigre put a blasted bullet in me. That's what's happened." He rose up on his elbows. "And now I'm turning state's evidence against him. I need the protection."

The man in the black suit smiled. "What the hell did you do to El Tigre? Steal one of his women?"

"Naw—I ran a big load for him, sold it, and kept the money for myself. And you know what? It was easy, *carnal*. A quarter mil—just like that." The man eased his body back down on the bed. "And now I need a big favor from you."

The man in black raised his eyebrows. "And what could I possibly do for you now that the government's got you in protective custody?"

"What you can do is go and find the money. I hid it in New Mexico—not far from here."

5

"Where in New Mexico?"

"Just across the state line—near a little one-horse town called Los Espíritus." The man hesitated and took a deep breath. "I buried it in what looked like an old Indian burial site, and I buried it real good. But when I went back to get it—it was gone."

"Do you think El Tigre got it?"

"Oh, hell no. I'm pretty sure a landowner found it—some guy who thinks he's a hotshot archeologist. That's all I've been able to figure out." The man turned and pointed to his bedside table. "There's a small piece of paper there. I've written the name of the landowner for you. With your contacts and your investigation savvy, you should be able to find my money."

The man in black leaned closer to the small man. "And what's in it for me?"

"I'll split it with you—fifty-fifty. Just keep my part until this El Tigre problem is over."

The man in black patted the small man on the shoulder. "I'll see what I can find out. I don't get down to New Mexico much anymore, but I guess I can do this for you." He hesitated, smiled, and said, "And—don't hold your breath." He picked up the piece of paper from the bedside table and walked out of the room.

Chapter One

Larissa Lasoya stomped her foot down on the accelerator. "Come on! Get on up this hill!" she screeched.

She disliked her sluggish van, and she hated the grueling trip to Perico Mesa just to bring supplies to Eloy Flores. But trips to the archeological dig site were part of her job duties. She clenched her teeth and held the accelerator down until she reached the top of the mesa.

After parking her van in the stand of ponderosa pines sheltering the team's camp, Larissa took a deep breath and looked toward the dig site. Surprisingly, she saw no one, not even the student assistants. This pleased Larissa and she smiled to herself. Perhaps she would not have to see the repulsive Eloy Flores at all. Since the first day she had met him, he had been making inappropriate advances toward her. Reporting his behavior to the head of their department had changed nothing. Because of this situation, Larissa had just completed a miserable first year of employment in the anthropology department at Santa Elena College.

Before opening her van door, Larissa took her fishing hat from where it lay on the seat. She quickly put it on and crammed her braids up under the crown. Most of the time she wore her long brown hair loose around her shoulders or held back at the nape of her neck.

With her hat in place, she got out and went to the back of the van and began unloading supplies. She glanced at the camp's large metal container holding the garbage she had to take back to Los Espíritus for disposal. She hoped it was bagged and ready to go.

As Larissa organized the supplies on the tables placed near a small camper trailer, she picked up a candy bar wrapper from the ground, folded it, and put it in the pocket of her faded jeans. She believed in keeping the dig sites free of litter and wished that Eloy and his student helpers were more conscientious. She wiped some of the sticky candy residue from her fingers with the bottom of her canary yellow tee shirt. Usually, she did not wear this shirt because she considered it too bright for her olive skin tone. It was something she wore when she really did not care how she looked, and today was one of those days. In fact, she hoped Eloy would find her appearance disgusting.

With the supplies unloaded, Larissa walked away from the camp toward a clearing just beyond the trees. She had noted this treeless area from previous times when she had brought supplies for the dig team. Now, the clearing piqued her interest and beckoned to her, enticing her to take a closer look. As she walked alone through the dark, cool shade of the forest, an uncanny sense of anticipation washed over her.

Walking northward, her eyes were drawn to the distant mountains rising above the river valley which separated El Perico Mesa from the higher mesas on the north and east. Stands of fir and ponderosa pine covered most of the land, with blue spruce growing sparingly in the valleys. Larissa closed her eyes and shivered.

As she emerged from the pines and entered the clearing, something drew her to the edge of the mesa. She continued and then suddenly stopped and caught her breath as her eyes fell upon a group of white tent rocks cascading down a steep incline. She stared at the formations below her, captivated by the towering cone-shaped rocks that reminded her of gigantic stone tepees. Motionless and barely breathing, Larissa delighted in the scene that lay before her. Never had she experienced such an extraordinary sight.

She inched closer to the edge of the mesa. As she stood there above the tent rocks, an eerie sensation swept over her as if something unseen had just passed through her body. Surprisingly, this did not frighten her; it was exhilarating. Suddenly, she was compelled to turn and look behind her. She gasped. A man was standing not more than ten feet from her. He held up his hand with the palm facing outward as if giving her a sign of friendship.

"I'm sorry if I frightened you." He lowered his hand. "I thought you heard me." He took a few steps toward her. "I'm looking for Dr. Eloy Flores."

The man appeared to be Native American, but Larissa was not certain. He was perhaps thirty-five years old, maybe a little younger. Larissa noted that he was quite a bit taller than her mere five-feet-two inches. He had on jeans, a western shirt, boots, and a wide-brimmed hat. His large Navajo silver belt buckle set with turquoise stones did not escape Larissa's eyes as she closely scrutinized the man. He wore his black hair in two long braids, and Larissa made a special mental note of this.

The man spoke again, "Where can I find Dr. Eloy Flores?"

"I'm not sure, but I know he and his assistants are somewhere here on the mesa because the college van is parked at their camp site." Larissa held out her hand. "My name is Larissa Lozoya, and I'm from the anthropology department at Santa Elena College."

The man shook her hand. "I'm Dr. Aaron Wolf. I've just been hired by the history department at your institution." He glanced down at the tent rocks and then back at Larissa. "Dr. Flores is a friend of mine."

She did not respond.

He then smiled at Larissa for the first time. "Are you admiring the village of the tribe of giants?" He pointed toward the tent rocks.

Actually, Larissa was admiring Dr. Aaron Wolf more than she was admiring anything else. "Yes, I find them very unusual. Have you ever seen anything like them before?" She kept her eyes on him.

He nodded. "Yes, I've seen some similar formations in other parts of New Mexico, but I've never seen these before. It's amazing what erosion can do to a mountain side."

Larissa nodded in agreement and, being determined to know more about Dr. Wolf, she said, "You look Native American, but you're not from any of our New Mexico tribes, are you?"

"I was born and raised in Oklahoma—my mother was Native American." He paused and asked, "Are you Mexican?"

"Well, I guess you could say I'm half-Mexican because my mother was originally from Mexico. My father's grandparents arrived here from Spain many years ago, but my father always insisted they were not Spanish. He said they were Basques and they didn't even speak Spanish." She shrugged her shoulders. "They had a sheep ranch east of here and . . . ."

Suddenly, Larissa quit talking. How foolish she must appear to this man. He did not seem to be listening to the rambling tale about her ancestry. He had turned his head toward the pine trees.

"Do you know where I should look for Eloy Flores?"

"I'm sorry I don't know." She motioned for Aaron Wolf to accompany her.

As they walked, side by side, back toward the stand of pines, Larissa detected the faint scent of bay rum. The unique odor seemed to be eliciting something from her memory, but it just would not come. This had happened to her on several occasions when she had smelled this distinctive woody fragrance. Now she found herself wanting to move closer to Aaron Wolf, to be nearer to the obvious source of the scent. Of course, she kept her distance.

Desiring to engage in conversation, Larissa asked, "Are you a medicine man? Your braids—that's why I asked, and also because I'm an inquisitive anthropologist."

"No, I'm not a medicine man. My braids are just a manifestation of my culture." He looked straight ahead.

11

"Mine, too." She laughed and pulled one of her long braids out from under her fishing hat, shook it, and then put it back under the hat. "Just a manifestation of *my* culture."

He seemed a little distant and did not respond to Larissa's antics. She asked him no more questions, and they walked silently into camp.

Eloy's student assistants José García and Marcos Sandoval were at the camp when Larissa and Aaron Wolf arrived, but Eloy was not to be seen.

After greeting both students, Larissa asked, "Where is Dr. Flores?"

"He's way over there." Marcos pointed to the south side of the large mesa. "He found something that looks like the remains of a man-made structure, and he got really excited about it. That's where we've been most of the day."

"I need one of you to please show this gentleman where he can find Dr. Flores." Larissa looked from one student to the other.

Marcos readily volunteered. Before Aaron Wolf left with the student, he thanked Larissa for her help.

Larissa quickly said, "You're welcome, and I'll see you at the College, Dr. Wolf. My office is in the museum building."

Aaron Wolf mumbled something, but Larissa did not understand him, and she did not want to bother to ask what he had said. She kept her eyes on him until he disappeared beyond some pines, and then she turned toward José.

"It's always good to see you, José."

The young man smiled but said nothing. He was one of Larissa's favorite students, and she was worried that he would have to drop out of school because of money problems.

Larissa pointed toward the supplies she had unloaded. "You need to secure the food I left on the camp table. But first, will you help me load the garbage?" She opened the back doors of her van. "You men are going to have to bring your final load of garbage yourselves as this is probably my last trip up here for the summer. With classes starting next week, I guess Dr. Flores will probably be closing the site soon."

José shook his head. "No, Dr. Lozoya. I don't think we'll be leaving next week." He looked at Larissa and frowned. "Dr. Flores says we still need two or three more months of work up here, and he wants to stay as long as we can before winter sets in." José began loading the bulging garbage bags. "I'll have to work long weekends here and still go to classes. You know, Dr. Flores says we can't just abandon this place until we've completed the work we've started."

Larissa made room in the van for the last bag of garbage. "I bet you don't want to be away from home much longer."

"It's not that I mind being here, I just don't like not being able to get any radio reception. Besides no music, we don't have any idea what's going on in the world until we make a trip back to Los Espíritus." José put the last bag into the van.

Larissa shrugged. "Well, most of the news isn't good anyway, just a lot about the war and the protests against our involvement in Vietnam. They've been burning American flags and draft cards. It's a mess." Larissa picked up a bottle cap from the ground.

José closed the back doors of the van and then turned toward Larissa. "Dr. Lozoya, I was wondering if there have been any protests on college campuses here in New Mexico."

"I haven't heard of any." Larissa looked toward the southern part of the large mesa. "José, did Dr. Flores have anything other than the garbage that needs to go back with me?"

"No, we haven't prepared anything for you to transport."

Larissa looked again toward the south. Then she said good-bye to José, got into her van, and headed back down the steep, winding road. All the way down to the highway, Aaron Wolf was on her mind, and all the way to Los Espíritus she could not get her thoughts off him. Thinking about the man with the two long braids helped ease the loneliness of the two-hour drive back down the river. She had made this trip a number of times and always enjoyed the beauty of this valley in the northern part of the state, but today she did not even notice when the aspen trees along the river gave way to giant cottonwoods and the ponderosa pines were replaced by *piñon* trees and junipers. Her thoughts were occupied with other things such as long, black braids and a silver belt buckle.

***

When Larissa arrived in Los Espíritus, thoughts of Aaron Wolf kept her from paying attention to the quaint and picturesque town nestled in a narrow river valley. She drove through the streets lined with adobe brick buildings, some of them more than a hundred and fifty years old, and she really did not see them. Picturing the face of Aaron Wolf with his high cheekbones, almond-shaped eyes, and full lips kept her mind busy. Most of all, that special thing about him grabbed her attention—something she especially liked—his braids.

Feeling a strong urge to discuss Aaron Wolf with her dearest confidant, Larissa drove directly to La Llorona Cantina and Dance Hall. She parked her van along the side of a small tree-lined plaza. The plaza, formerly abandoned during the day, now had become a regular hangout for a group of young individuals who were referred to by some people as hippies. Their arrival in Los Espíritus puzzled many of the local citizens, and some considered the hippies a nuisance. Larissa paid little attention to the newcomers, but she thought it strange for young women to go without their bras in public.

As a child, Larissa had played in this plaza while her father took care of his half-interest in the cantina. The plaza's circular-shaped gazebo with its concrete floor had been a wonderful place for her to roller skate. She had sat on, jumped off, and hid under the very same wrought-iron bench where three young women were now sitting. As Larissa got out of her van, several of these braless women waved at her. She greeted the women, and then walked quickly across the street to the large, adobe-brick building housing the cantina and dance hall. Her late father's half-interest in the business now belonged to Larissa, although the actual hands-on management of the establishment had been left to his partner Mimi Geller.

Larissa pushed opened the heavy, carved wooden door and walked into the dark and cavernous cantina. Being early afternoon, there were few patrons sitting at the tables placed around the high-ceilinged room. A beer sign on the wall next to the cue stick rack flashed its colored neon lights. Larissa went up to the massive mahogany bar and jumped up onto one of the stools. She smiled broadly at the large, bald-headed man behind the bar.

"Hello, my dear Braulio." Larissa took her fishing hat off and laid it on the bar.

The big man smiled at her, showing the absence of front teeth, both upper and lower. He had never replaced them since he had lost them in the Bataan Death March during the Second World War. Braulio had never married, and some people swore he had been castrated with a bayonet during the time of his imprisonment by the Japanese. In spite of the inhuman things that may have been done to him, Braulio maintained a happy and outgoing disposition.

"Hello, *mi reina*." He reached across the bar and enveloped both of Larissa's hands in one of his large hands, and then he gently touched the end of her slightly turned up nose with his index finger.

16

It delighted Larissa when the man called her his queen. Sometimes he called her his beautiful brown-eyed girl, something he had done since her childhood.

Larissa pointed toward the large jar of pickled pig feet sitting on the back bar. "May I please have a *pata*? I'm so hungry."

Braulio took tongs and fished out a pig foot for her and wrapped it in a piece of wax paper.

"*Bon appétit*," he said as he laid the delicacy in front of Larissa. He then turned and poured her a glass of ginger ale. "You never drink milk anymore. I think you should."

Larissa frowned. "Braulio, I'm a grown woman. I don't like milk."

She took a big swallow of the ginger ale. Then she began slowly savoring the pig foot, allowing some of its gelatinous substance to run down her chin. As Braulio washed beer mugs, Larissa watched him and thought of how he had been a big part of her life. Several times he had pulled her out of the creek behind the building when she had fallen in while trying to coax crawfish out of the water with bacon tied on pieces of string. It usually had been Braulio who had helped her with her homework on the nights she had stayed with Mimi in the apartment adjoining the cantina. Although Mimi had completed medical school in Germany, the unschooled Braulio had been more successful at tutoring Larissa, especially in math.

Just as Larissa asked for another glass of ginger ale, Mimi came through the doorway from her apartment. Her emerald green dress accentuated her flaming red hair, and her collection of gold bangle bracelets jangled as she walked.

"Larissa, you're here early! I didn't expect you back from up north so soon." Mimi's smile created hundreds of wrinkles, yet the remnant of a beautiful woman could still be seen in the heavily made-up face.

"I didn't stay very long." Larissa had finished eating the best part of the pig foot and now began sucking on the knuckle bones.

Mimi took a seat on the bar stool next to Larissa. "Braulio, pour me a cup of coffee, please."

Mimi spoke English with the accent she had never lost since escaping Nazi Germany with her late husband Hiram in the 1930's. She and Hiram had been physicians in Germany, but Mimi never returned to her profession once she arrived in New Mexico. She said managing the cantina always kept her busy and content.

Mimi took a sip of her coffee. "Braulio, did those hippie girls come back in here today?"

Braulio looked down. "Yes. They wanted ice water again, and to use the toilet."

"Well, don't give them any more ice water. And they need to buy something if they're going to be using the facilities." Mimi shook her head. "They're disgusting."

Larissa laughed. "I saw three of them sitting in the plaza. They aren't wearing bras, and I could see their nipples through those thin little undershirts they're wearing."

"Ha! They may look good now, but young teats need support. Just wait until they're forty.

18

Their nipples will be dragging on the ground!" Mimi snorted and slapped the top of the bar with her open palm.

Larissa laughed again, and then wrapped the remains of the pig foot in the wax paper, handed it to Braulio, and then quickly wiped her face and hands. "Mimi, I want to tell you what happened to me today." Larissa hesitated and sighed. "I met a man."

The older woman said nothing but stared unblinkingly at Larissa. Braulio appeared to be busy, but Larissa suspected that he always listened to what she and Mimi talked about.

Larissa continued, "The man seemed very unusual. I can't explain it."

Braulio looked up quickly. "What do you mean?"

Larissa shrugged her shoulders. "I felt a little peculiar being near him. I guess it was the scent of his aftershave that made me want to remember something, but I'm not sure what." Larissa sighed again. "Mimi, I found him fascinating, and I couldn't stop looking at him."

"Who is he? What did he want?" Mimi frowned and took a drink of her coffee.

"He's Dr. Aaron Wolf from Oklahoma, and the history department has just hired him, and I think he's very handsome." Larissa took a deep breath. "He has two braids, like mine, and I've never been attracted to men with long hair." Larissa looked around the room to make sure there were no men with long hair who might have overheard her.

19

Mimi held out her cup for Braulio to pour more coffee. "Larissa, you'd better not tell Carmelita what you just told me about being attracted to this stranger from Oklahoma, or that old Yaqui witch will be preparing love potions for you to give that poor man." Mimi shook a well-manicured finger at Larissa. "No, you don't want to tell Carmelita about him."

Carmelita, the maid who had come to Los Espíritus from Mexico years before with Larissa's mother, seemed to think of herself as a great sorceress. For decades the old woman had been reading Tarot cards and mixing herbs and potions for the lovelorn of Los Espíritus. On many occasions, Carmelita had been applying her arcane skills when she should have been cleaning house or doing the laundry.

Larissa laughed at what Mimi had just said about Carmelita, and then she gulped down the remainder of her ginger ale.

Mimi reached over and put her hand on Larissa's arm. "Maybe you do need one of Carmelita's love potions. I think it's time you fell in love. My God, you're almost thirty-one years old already! Before you know it you'll be too old to have babies." Mimi frowned and looked intently at Larissa. "And I'm tired of telling you this."

"But you already know I'm too busy for love and marriage and babies." Larissa picked up her fishing hat and slid off the bar stool. "Besides, I've never met a man I wanted to do you know what with."

Mimi set her coffee cup down and turned to face Larissa. "Where are you going so quickly?"

"I'm going home to see if Carmelita is still there. I need to talk to her about a man and a love potion." Larissa laughed loudly and said good-bye.

Chapter Two

Larissa stood up, stretched, and then sat back down. She twisted and turned her body several times attempting to find a comfortable position at her desk. For most of the morning, she had worked off and on at filling out requisition forms for materials for the museum's dioramas. She considered herself fortunate to be occupying the only office in the refurbished building that housed the College's anthropology museum. This meant fewer interruptions during the day. But today she could not focus on her work.

From time to time, Larissa arose from her desk and moved around stretching her legs and trying to relax her mind. Several times she had lingered at the window looking out over the campus of red-brick buildings set among fir and spruce trees. How pleasant it should have been to be living at home again in Los Espíritus and to be employed by the College. However, her problem with Eloy Flores spoiled what otherwise could have been an ideal situation. She considered the short, stocky man overbearing and certainly not to her liking. It was difficult for Larissa to understand how anyone could be so inappropriate to a colleague. And, furthermore, Eloy had a wife.

As Larissa was looking out her window, Eloy Flores entered her office without knocking as usual. Larissa started toward her desk in an attempt to put it between her and Eloy, but he reached her too quickly. Grabbing her wrists and backing her up against the wall, he attempted to kiss her. She pushed him away and quickly moved across the room.

"Oh, come on, Larissa. You're such a pretty little thing. I can't keep my hands off of you." Eloy leered at Larissa and began slowly inching toward her.

Moving in behind her desk, Larissa picked up the telephone receiver. "Eloy, get out of my office, or I'm calling campus security!"

Eloy stopped, narrowed his eyes, and glared at her. "If you want to keep your job here, you won't report anything to anybody. You had better remember that, little lady."

Larissa continued holding the telephone receiver in her hand while she stood staring at the graying, middle-aged man.

Then with what sounded like an affected tone of dejection, Eloy said, "*Mi amor*, I just came to tell you there's mail for you in the department office. Do you want me to bring it to you?"

"No, I'll go get my own mail. And for the millionth time—quit calling me your love." Larissa put the telephone receiver down because Eloy had begun backing toward the doorway.

"I'll be nice to you, *mi amor*. But you need to be nicer to me." Eloy laughed and walked out of Larissa's office.

Larissa sat down at her desk and took several deep breaths. What more could she do? Reporting Eloy to Dr. Pete Ríos, their immediate supervisor, had not stopped Eloy's behavior. Larissa hesitated to take the matter to a higher authority for fear of not being believed. No one had ever witnessed Eloy touching her because he always seemed to be cautious. Furthermore, Eloy had tenure with the College and Larissa, having just signed her second year contract, was still on probation. If she created a big fuss about Eloy, she feared she would lose her job.

Larissa arose from her desk and looked out her window toward the faculty parking lot. She noticed a man placing items into a cardboard box as he stood at the tailgate of a pickup. He wore jeans, a western shirt, and a wide-brimmed hat. When Larissa saw the man's braids, she smiled. *He's probably moving into his office*, she mused as she stood at her window and observed the man who had so intensely interested her at El Perico Mesa. She watched as he carried a box into the adjacent building which housed faculty and department offices.

Larissa reluctantly returned to her work, but found focusing on her tasks difficult because she kept walking over to the window to look out at Aaron Wolf's pickup. When she noticed Aaron Wolf came out of the building and head toward the back of his pickup, Larissa contemplated offering to help him move into his office.

Actually, she did not want to help him at all, but she did want to interact with him again. And most importantly, she wanted to show him she could look pretty and feminine instead of unkempt and boyish as she had appeared when she encountered him at El Perico Mesa. Today would be an excellent day to do this because she was wearing a peasant blouse and a red, full skirt, and red seemed to be one of Larissa's best colors. Also, she had put on makeup and curled her hair. Today she had no braids stuffed up under a dirty fishing hat. So, with a feeling of confidence, she quickly left the museum and walked out to the parking lot.

"Hello, Dr. Wolf," Larissa said as she neared the back of his pickup.

He looked up at her and nodded his head.

She walked up to him smiling. "Welcome to Santa Elena College. I see you're moving into your office. Do you need any help carrying your things?"

He had a pleasant look on his face, but he did not really smile at Larissa. "No thank you, I've already finished." He closed the pickup's tailgate.

"That's good. Then may I take you to lunch if you have no other plans?" Larissa had not intended to say this, but it just came out of her mouth.

Aaron Wolf hesitated and looked away for a moment and then looked back at her. "No thank you. I have a policy of not dating students."

What he said surprised her, and suddenly she realized he had not recognized her. "Well, it sounds like a good policy. It should keep you out of trouble." She smiled at him. "I hope you don't have the same policy regarding your colleagues."

He looked somewhat puzzled but did not respond.

Larissa made no further comments about his dating policies. She also ignored the fact he had not recognize her. This way she hoped he would not be too embarrassed when he realized his mistake.

"Well, again, let me say welcome, Dr. Wolf. And when you have time, come by the museum and see what we have accomplished." Larissa smiled and walked away forcing herself not to look back at him. She went directly to the museum, locked the doors, and began the two-block walk to her house.

***

Carmelita, having just made a bean taco and a glass of *horchata* for Larissa's lunch, was sitting in the kitchen when Larissa arrived home. Larissa kissed the short, gray-haired woman on her brown, wrinkled cheek, and, kicking off her shoes, sat down at the kitchen table.

Carmelita raised her left eyebrow and looked sternly at Larissa. "Why do you have such a peculiar look on your face, *muchacha*?"

"Do I look peculiar to you? *Lo siento*, I'm sorry." Larissa usually tried to ignore Carmelita's gaze, especially when the older woman let her right eyelid droop almost shut.

"*¡Válgame Dios!* You can't fool me. I've known you since the day you were born. Something's going on with you." The elderly woman stood up, and placing her gnarled hands on her hips, looked intently with her only good eye at Larissa.

Larissa laid her taco back on her plate. "I've just talked to a man for the second time and he makes me feel tingly all over—and that's what's going on with me."

"I knew it, I knew it! *Madre de Dios*, I knew it had to be a man!" Carmelita laughed. "Tell me about how he makes you feel."

"Well, it's like there's something mystifying about the scent of his shampoo or aftershave or something. It affects me, but I can't explain it." Larissa picked up her glass and took a sip of *horchata*. "And I wanted to reach out and touch him, and just looking at him made me feel good all over."

"*¡Ay, La Purísima de María!* Your spirit has united with its spirit mate!" Carmelita patted Larissa's arm with her brown, wrinkled hand. "You're very lucky to have met this man. I'll light candles for you."

"Wait a minute! What's a spirit mate?" Larissa laughed. "It sounds like some of your hocus-pocus baloney." She picked up the taco and quickly began eating it.

Carmelita looked hurt as she usually did when Larissa questioned her wisdom.

The older woman sat down at the table across from Larissa and shook a finger at her. "When you meet a stranger and you feel a prior connection to him, it's because your spirits know one another." Carmelita reached over and brushed a tiny piece of refried bean from Larissa's blouse. "And if you have an urge to touch this man, it's because your spirits have already been in love for a long, long time—perhaps even before you were born."

Larissa swallowed the last of her taco. "Well, I'm not sure if I feel any previous connection with this man, and I've never heard you talk about my spirit mate before. Maybe I should take field notes."

Carmelita closed her eyes. "You and this man will find it easy to fall in love because now you and your spirits are reunited." Then she opened her eyes and looked intently at Larissa.

"My goodness, Carmelita, do you think this man knows what his spirit and my spirit have been doing behind our backs?" Larissa tried to keep from laughing to avoid hurting Carmelita.

"I'll tell you what is going to happen." Carmelita pointed her finger at Larissa again. "You and he will fall deeply in love. It is destiny, and you can't stop it. When he looked at you, he felt the same thing you were feeling." Carmelita sighed, then stood up and picked up Larissa's empty plate.

Larissa slightly smiled, more to herself than to Carmelita. "Well, I hope you are correct! I think I'd like a love affair with this man." She wiped her mouth with a nearby dish towel.

Carmelita set the empty plate back on the table and narrowed her dark eyes. "But I must warn you. There are three who will attempt to keep you apart, two men and a woman. Beware of them."

Larissa slipped her shoes back onto her feet and stood up. "Wow! It sounds as if you've been messing around with your Tarot cards again."

Carmelita wrinkled her brow and slowly shook her head. "The cards don't lie. I'm worried for you."

"All of this sounds exciting, Carmelita, my dear. Thanks for lunch, and will you make some chicken enchiladas with green chili sauce? Maybe I'll bring someone home tonight for supper."

"I hope, if it's a man, he's a decent man and not married, *muchacha*. You better make sure first." Carmelita raised her left eyebrow. "Don't forget, some men are *cabrones*."

"The one I'm bringing home is not married. I've already asked his department secretary. She assured me he is single, and the department secretaries know everything about everybody."

Carmelita patted Larissa's arm. "I'll make the enchiladas with green chili sauce, a very *special* chili sauce, just for you and the man you are bringing home."

All the way back to her office, Carmelita's words played around in Larissa's mind. Larissa wondered if Aaron Wolf had felt tingly all over when he had looked at her. She hoped he had, but she seriously doubted he had felt anything. In fact, she did not believe much of what Carmelita had told her during lunch. But, on the other hand, Carmelita was almost always correct in her prophecies.

***

On arriving back at the museum, Larissa returned to her task of ordering the materials she needed, but she could not put Aaron Wolf out of her mind. As she worked, she tried to design a plan to entice him to come to her house for supper. Perhaps she should just telephone him at his office and invite him. No—this might be too forward, and he would probably decline her invitation. Maybe she should go to his office to say hello and see what might transpire. She would ask him for a ride home.

Yes, she would do this just as soon as she finished the remainder of her tasks for the day.

Larissa worked at her desk for over three hours, stopping occasionally to look out the window at Aaron Wolf's pickup in the parking lot. Just as she was completing her tasks, the back door of the museum loudly opened, and Aaron Wolf suddenly appeared in the doorway of her office.

"Dr. Lozoya, I came to apologize for not recognizing you this morning."

Larissa looked up. He was smiling at her. She caught her breath and felt her heart beating rapidly.

She smiled and took a deep breath before saying, "It's okay. I can certainly understand why you didn't recognize me. I looked like a street urchin when you saw me at El Perico Mesa." She motioned for Aaron to come into her office.

He stepped in. "I made the comment about not dating students only because I mistook you for a student."

"Well, I guess it must be a compliment if you think I look as young as most of our students." Larissa pointed to a chair, but he continued standing. "And, Dr. Wolf, you never responded to my comment about your policy on dating colleagues. Maybe you haven't formulated a policy yet." Larissa laughed, hoping he would think she had spoken in jest. She really had not.

He shrugged his shoulders. "I really don't date. I don't have much to offer because I have a lot of financial responsibilities in my life right now."

Larissa smiled. "I can understand that, and I myself am not interested in any relationships because I'm so involved in my work." She turned away from him for a few moments only because she had not taken her eyes from him since he came to her doorway, and she did not want him to think she was inspecting him too closely. "It's been only a year since I came to work here. I have two more years to get this small museum developed and operating." She stood up. "If you have time, let me show you what we've completed so far."

He followed her out into the main room where she showed him the locked display cases which held a few artifacts.

"As you can see, I still have a lot of empty cases to fill. Of course, there are some interesting items from the site at El Perico Mesa needing to be catalogued and prepared for display. We have them locked in the work room." She pointed to a door adjacent to her office.

Aaron Wolf walked along the glass display cases looking at several baskets, some tools, and a few items of pottery. "And the dioramas, what will they depict?" He pointed to the far side of the room.

Larissa motioned for him to follow her, and she began explaining the four dioramas which were in progress.

"There will be scenes from each of the early native cultures from this geographical area. We've almost completed the Paleo-Indian and the Archaic dioramas, and we'll soon be starting the Basket Maker and the Pueblo. Eventually we will subdivide the cultures appropriately and display them all the way around two walls."

Aaron looked at the glass-enclosed dioramas. "Those look very nice. You must be an artist."

"No, not at all—the art department is involved in the project."

He turned toward her. "Who's in charge of all of this?"

"Well, I designed the overall concept for the museum. Of course, our department head, Dr. Pete Ríos, had input into the plans. Primarily, along with student helpers, I clean and prepare the artifacts. We also identify the objects, do the research, catalog them, and write the text for the displays."

"Are there any Native Americans involved in the development of your museum?" His eyes riveted hers.

She hesitated before answering. "None at this time." She looked away from him.

"Don't you find that a little strange?"

She looked back at him and, fixing her eyes on his, quietly said, "Dr. Wolf, I find a lot of things in this world strange, as well as unjust and unfair. And I certainly think Native Americans should be in charge of their own museums just as they should be in charge of their own destinies. However, I am an anthropologist, a scientist, and all I can do is be as unbiased as possible when I examine the aspects of a culture—any culture."

"How did you get interested in all of this?" His words reflected a serious tone.

"My father was an amateur archeologist, so I've lived among artifacts all my life. I've become highly interested in the people who used the objects which have been left behind."

Aaron Wolf said nothing and moved away from her, continuing to study the dioramas.

Then he turned back. "I guess you'd really like to dig up some of my ancestors, wouldn't you?"

She stopped, and with a forced smile on her face, replied, "Not at all, Dr. Wolf. I'd really rather dig into you."

He took a step backwards. "What do you mean?"

"I mean, right now I'm more interested in you than any of your dead relatives. I'd like to know about your world view, how you relate to your environment, and what you think about things, like our presence in Vietnam." She smiled again.

He frowned. "Why do you want to know anything about me?"

"Because I'm an anthropologist. Why don't you start with your interests?"

His frown disappeared. "Well, of course my interest is American history, and specifically the history of the first civilizations on this continent. I'm especially interested in the Pueblo culture."

She did not like mentioning Eloy's name, but she said, "I guess you know Eloy Flores is an expert on the Anasazi culture and their descendants. And he can tell you a lot about the Pueblo people and their history."

"Yes, I've known Eloy since he taught in Oklahoma when I was doing my undergraduate degree. He had invited me to the dig site at El Perico Mesa on the day I met you." Aaron turned and began slowly walking back along the row of dioramas.

It delighted Larissa to hear what he had just said about his interest in the Pueblo culture. Now she had a reasonable ploy to lure him to her house. She was eager to know him better, and, up to now, she had found him fascinating.

"Dr. Wolf, I want to offer you some resources. At my house I have some old photos, a number of documents, and two diaries relating to Pueblo history." She followed behind him.

He turned and Larissa saw what she thought was a look of interest on his face.

She continued, "My father acquired these items over the years. I'm planning to donate them to our museum, but, if you like, you can see them first to determine if they would be of interest to you." She hesitated.

Aaron Wolf moved closer toward her.

She watched him intently. "I'm sure you could probably squeeze several journal articles out of the diaries alone. That should definitely help you in your pursuit of tenure with the College." She took a deep breath and fixed her eyes on his face. "Would you like to come to my house and look at these photos and documents and eat some green enchiladas with me?"

He now stood very close to Larissa. "When? Do you mean now?" He seemed to be a little surprised, and perhaps a little hesitant.

"Yes, in fact, I thought you could give me a ride home as soon as I'm finished here, unless you have something else planned." She looked at her watch. "It's getting late. You would really be doing me a favor. About the ride, I mean."

He shrugged and said, "Sure, I owe you something for not recognizing you today. I'm ready to go whenever you are."

Elated, Larissa quickly went into her office and cleared her desk, locked the building, and followed Aaron Wolf to his pickup. He opened the passenger-side door for her and she got in. She ran her hand over the fabric of the seat between where she sat and where he would soon be seated. Then she smelled it—the faint fragrance of bay rum. She closed her eyes and took a deep breath. The scent again hinted at something deep down in the darkness of her memories. No matter how hard she tried, she could not bring it to the surface. Her breathing became shallow and her heart seemed to be beating faster than usual.

When Aaron Wolf got into the cab of the pickup, Larissa had the uncanny sensation that she was where she should be, sitting next to him. Perhaps the power of suggestion had affected her mind. After all, Carmelita had told her the ridiculous story about Aaron's spirit and her spirit being in love. Larissa hoped Carmelita had made a pan of enchiladas. And she hoped Carmelita had made them with her very *special* green chili sauce.

Chapter Three

Aaron Wolf started the engine of his pickup and smiled at Larissa. "I'm looking forward to your green enchiladas. I think I forgot to eat lunch today."

"Well then, it's a good thing I invited you to take a look at my father's materials." Larissa sat back and tried to relax.

"Which way to your house?" he asked.

Larissa attempted to appear nonchalant as she pointed for him to turn left as they exited the parking lot. "I live only two blocks from campus, so I seldom bring my vehicle."

She felt an unusual anticipation as she sat on the seat next to Aaron Wolf. Her voice seemed a little shaky as she gave him directions to her house. She tried to control herself and hoped he did not detect anything unusual. Never in all her life had she responded to a man this way, and she relished in the exhilaration she was feeling.

"Do you live alone?" he asked.

"Yes. My father died recently. I never knew my mother, and I have no siblings," Larissa said as they turned down a narrow street leading away from the back side of the campus. "And I've never been married either," she added.

"I guess you've lived in Los Espíritus all of your life," he said.

"I was born here, but my father sent me to Dallas to boarding school during my teen years. I stayed in New Mexico for my university degrees." She hesitated a moment and pointed toward her house. "I live there. Park your pickup in the driveway."

Aaron Wolf turned into a long driveway lined with tall cottonwoods. A double-car garage sat at the far end of the driveway. Aaron took off his hat and left it on the seat and followed Larissa to the front porch of the large adobe house. She unlocked the carved wooden door and invited Aaron Wolf in. As they entered, a yellow cat roused from his nap on the sofa and meowed.

"This is King Carlos the Ninth." Larissa walked over to the animal and stroked his back. "All of our cats have been named King Carlos. My father had King Carlos the First when he married my mother, and he just kept naming each subsequent cat the same name. I guess you can say the first one has had nine lives because, after thirty something years, here he is again as number nine."

"Interesting," Aaron Wolf said, and he looked around the large living room with its high ceiling of herringbone design between the round pine *vigas*. "I see someone killed a bear." He pointed down at the bear-skin rug lying on the wool carpet in front of a large fireplace.

"My father killed the bear many years ago. It was either he or the bear according to the story my father told." Larissa shuddered. "My father encountered the bear in a deep ravine while hunting deer. The bear reared up and threatened him, so my father shot it."

Aaron Wolf frowned. "Oh, and did he eat the bear's flesh?"

"I don't think so. I never remember eating bear meat— just venison and elk." Larissa pointed to several mounted deer heads on the wall, and then she sighed deeply. "I've asked Brother Bear many times to forgive my father, and I think he has."

"I've never killed anything I didn't intend to eat," Aaron Wolf said as he stood frowning and looking down at the bear rug.

Larissa thought she detected a hint of disapproval from him, and she hesitated a moment before speaking. "Well, I hope you like to eat green enchiladas. But, first, let me show you the old photos and documents."

Aaron Wolf followed Larissa through the living room and into the adjoining dining room. On the large oak dining table sat a small basket.

He stopped and looked at it. "May I pick it up?" he asked.

"Yes, but hold it with the cloth it's sitting on."

He took the basket in his hands and turned it in several directions.

Larissa said, "It's Yavapai Apache, late nineteenth century."

"It's unique." He set the basket down. "Did you buy it from an Apache?"

"No, my father traded for it. I have it here on the table because I need to clean it. I'm going to donate it to the museum."

Larissa motioned for him to follow her. She led him through the kitchen and then through a doorway leading into a large room at the back of the house. The mahogany paneled den had one entire wall of shelves filled with pottery, baskets, and other Native American items. A desk and a large four-poster bed took up the other side of the room. One of the den's corners accommodated a small adobe fireplace. Next to it, an exterior door gave access to the back courtyard. Two other doors concealed a closet and a small bathroom. The den had no windows.

"That's a big bed for a small person such as you," Aaron said.

"Oh, I don't ever sleep in this bed. There are two bedrooms off the hall by the dining room. One of those is mine. I don't use this room at all. I prefer to work at the dining room table."

Aaron stood looking around the den. "And what about the large door?" He nodded toward the exterior door.

"It goes outside." Larissa opened the door so he could see the courtyard and the apartment attached to the back of the garage.

He nodded toward the garage apartment. "I guess you have a big storage room out there filled with Native American artifacts."

"No, it's just an apartment. My father usually kept it rented to college students. It's not rented now." Larissa closed the door and locked it.

"This is a very nice den. It's too bad you don't use it." Aaron walked over to a standing glass display case containing two feather-covered garments. "Where did you get these?"

"I'm not sure. They've been here ever since I can remember. My father kept them in a drawer before he put them in this case several years ago."

"They look like burial robes, and the small one belonged to a baby." Aaron hesitated a moment, and then turned toward Larissa. "Who robbed the graves to get these?" He had a grim look on his face.

"I don't know, and I don't approve of robbing graves or plundering archeological sites. I would never do such a thing." She turned away from his gaze and pointed to a file cabinet. "I'm going to heat our enchiladas while you look in this drawer. You are hungry, aren't you?"

"Yes, I am." He walked over to the file cabinet.

Larissa went into the kitchen and lit the oven and put a pot of coffee on the stove. Carmelita had left a pan of enchiladas in the refrigerator with a note on top in her childlike handwriting. It read, *NO COMES TANTAS*, meaning Larissa should not eat too many of the enchiladas. Laughing quietly to herself, Larissa threw the note into the garbage can and put the pan of enchiladas on the counter. On top of the stove, she heated the green chili sauce in a pot and added one of her own special ingredients. Then she poured the sauce over the enchiladas and put them into the oven to heat. Before going back to the den to join Aaron, she set two places on the table in the dining room.

When she returned to the den, Aaron Wolf looked up at her and said, "Well, Dr. Lozoya, these photos and documents are a treasure trove. In fact, they are priceless. Could I come another time and more carefully examine everything in the drawer? And I need to make notes."

41

She smiled, nodded, and then said, "Listen, you need to call me Larissa. If we're going to be colleagues and eat enchiladas together, we need to be on a first-name basis. Don't you think so, Aaron?"

"Sure, why not?" He walked back over to the feather burial robes. "These still bother me. I can't help but wonder what happened to the human remains which these robes once shrouded. Grave robbing bothers me."

"Yes, I know. And so does killing animals if you don't intend to eat them. Well, it bothers me, too." Larissa sounded a little forceful. "Does this surprise you?"

Aaron turned and faced her. "Not exactly, but I realize you probably think differently because you're not Native American."

"Oh, so you think only Native Americans have great reverence for the dead, as well as for all living things. Do you have the franchise on those beliefs?"

"That's not what I meant." Aaron seemed a little flustered.

Larissa sighed. "My mother was a *mestiza*, so I am definitely part Indian."

"Yes, I thought you might be when I first met you. But you said you never knew your mother. Her not raising you would have made a difference." Aaron raised his eyebrows.

"You're so right. It made a big difference because a Yaqui Indian by the name of Carmelita raised me. She came from Sonora, Mexico, with my mother when my parents married." Larissa laughed and took Aaron by the arm. "Come on. Let's eat some of Carmelita's green enchiladas. She's now the wife of a local man, so she's had to learn to cook like a New Mexican."

"Does Carmelita still cook for you? I thought you made the enchiladas." He followed Larissa into the dining room.

"She still looks after me for a few hours every day. She and her husband live nearby."

Larissa showed Aaron where to sit and then went to get the pan out of the oven.

From the kitchen, she said, "And, for your information, I can make delicious enchiladas. Carmelita has taught me how to cook. In fact, she's taught me how to do many things." Before Larissa walked out of the kitchen, she said under her breath, "And some of those things might surprise you."

Larissa served the enchiladas and poured two cups of coffee. They ate quietly, not saying much. She did ask Aaron if he had heard the news about the recent demonstrations against the war in Vietnam. He said he had read about it. Larissa said she feared the students at Santa Elena might engage in similar activities. He seemed to think the local students were a lot less radical than those involved in the demonstrations.

Aaron said he liked the enchiladas, and proceeded to eat four of them. All during the meal, Larissa found she could not keep from staring at him. Something about him captivated her. Never before in her life had she been so fascinated by a person, and she certainly had never been attracted to men with long hair. But there across from her sat

Aaron Wolf with two long braids and Larissa was enchanted with him.

As she picked at her food, Larissa fantasized about taking out his braids and running her hands through his hair. She stared at his face, at his dark brown eyes, and at his mouth. She felt a strong urge to reach out and touch him, but she did not, and she hardly ate any of Carmelita's enchiladas.

"I enjoyed the meal, Larissa. Thank you. I really like the taste of green chili." Aaron laid his fork down on his plate. "Especially Carmelita's New Mexico green chili."

His voice brought Larissa's mind back to the meal. "Oh, I'm glad to hear that. I'll tell Carmelita what you said." Larissa added a spoonful of sugar to her coffee and looked up at Aaron. "I've told you so much about myself, and I don't really know very much about you, other than what you told me at El Perico Mesa."

"I don't know what else to tell you. My parents died young, so my two sisters and I were raised by our grandmother in Oklahoma. I've always lived in a house, never in a tepee." He laughed and held his cup out to Larissa, and she poured him more coffee. "I received all of my education in Oklahoma. Eloy Martínez stimulated my interest in the Pueblo culture." Aaron added some canned milk to his coffee. "I took several anthropology courses with Eloy when he taught in Oklahoma, and he invited me about ten years ago to do some field work with him in southern Colorado." Aaron paused and took a sip of coffee. "As for

44

Santa Elena College, I'm hoping to develop ethnic studies syllabi."

Larissa said nothing for a few moments to give Aaron a chance to continue talking, but when he did not go on, she said, "Our department is fortunate to have several nearby sites we can investigate. I think we'll be going to a site in southern Colorado this coming summer."

"Do you work the sites?"

"No, I don't participate in the actual digs. But I do take supplies to the team and pick up anything needing to go back to the department—artifacts usually and the garbage always. I bought a used van because I needed room for carrying things." She folded her napkin and laid it on the table. "Primarily, I do the artifact research and cataloging. And I teach an anthropology class."

Aaron looked at his watch. "It's getting late. Thank you for the meal. I enjoyed the evening with you and King Carlos." He reached down and stroked the cat as it rubbed against his legs. Then Aaron stood up and put his chair back under the table.

Larissa smiled. "Thank you for the ride home, and you didn't owe me anything for not recognizing me today." She got up and followed Aaron to the living room.

Aaron stopped at the front door and turned and faced Larissa. "I hope I didn't offend you about the burial robes."

"It's okay, Aaron. I feel the same as you do." She stopped for a moment and slowly shook her head. "I would take those robes back where they

45

came from if I could. But I can't because I don't know where to take them. I've decided to clean them and donate them to the museum, along with everything else you saw on the shelves and in the file drawer." She looked deeply into his eyes. "I want to show respect for all cultures by properly and legitimately working with their artifacts."

Aaron reached down and took Larissa's hand. "Thank you again for the enchiladas, and tell Carmelita I said she makes delicious green chili sauce." He raised Larissa's hand and lightly brushed the back of it with his lips. "And forgive me for not recognizing you today." He slowly put her hand down and released it, then opened the door and walked out.

Larissa stood motionless, staring at the back of her hand. She felt a slight tingling where Aaron's lips had touched her skin. Had she not been scrutinizing her hand so intently, she might have seen Aaron walking to his pickup and rubbing his lips lightly with his index finger. She also might have seen him turn on the interior light in his pickup cab and look into the rearview mirror at his lips before he started the engine. Perhaps she would have guessed he was speculating about the tingling sensation he felt on his lips. But Larissa wasn't aware of any of this because she was too busy smiling and enjoying what she was feeling on the back of her hand.

Chapter Four

It was late autumn and Larissa, for the most part, was enjoying the cooler days. However, today had not been enjoyable because she had endured a headache for most of the afternoon. Aspirins had done nothing for her, so she stopped her work early and walked home. As she came across her front yard, she made a mental note that the leaves which had fallen from the cottonwoods needed raking.

On entering the living room, Larissa found Carmelita making a small fire in the fireplace, the first one of the season.

Larissa quickly crossed the room, dropped down onto the sofa, and stretched out on her back. "*Ay*, Carmelita, my head is killing me. Give me something please."

"Wait a minute. I need to get this fire going. There's a chill in the house, and I feel in my bones a snow storm is coming." The elderly woman continued her labor at the fireplace.

Larissa lay on the sofa looking up at the herringbone-patterned ceiling thinking about what she had to do the next day. Dr. Ríos had requested she take her van up to El Perico Mesa and help Eloy break camp for the season. Instead of stopping when the fall semester had started, the archeological team had continued working the site. Several students had been helping Eloy, and they had been taking turns staying in camp. As Larissa stared at the patterns on the ceiling, she realized she did not really want to help Eloy bring the equipment and supplies back to the College.

"*M'ija*, drink this tea." Carmelita interrupted Larissa's thoughts as she held out a cup of her special headache cure.

Larissa took the cup and began sipping the tea. When Larissa had finished drinking the special brew, she handed the cup to Carmelita. "My head still hurts."

Carmelita sat down on the sofa and placed Larissa's head in her lap. She began softly kneading the younger woman's head with her gnarled fingers while chanting words which held special meaning for Larissa and the elderly woman. Carmelita continued this ritual until Larissa fell asleep.

The next morning Larissa awakened with a small twinge of a headache. Dreading any interaction with Eloy, she decided not to make the trip to El Perico Mesa. It would be easy to telephone Dr. Ríos and tell him she felt too sick to go. She walked into her bedroom to make the phone call, but then hesitated. An unfamiliar sensation coursed through her body. Suddenly, she changed her mind. Something was compelling her to go— something she did not understand. She quickly got ready, put what she needed into her van, and left Los Espíritus.

As Larissa traveled the isolated road to El Perico Mesa, she listened to music on her van radio. Occasionally an announcer would give a one-minute synopsis of the news. Most of it seemed to be about the fighting in Vietnam. Larissa hated hearing about the protests and demonstrations against the war. This concerned her greatly, and she did not know for sure how she felt about the issues.

By the time she stopped at La Zorilla, she was no longer able to receive radio reception. La Zorilla was nothing more than a gasoline station and several old adobe buildings. Larissa stopped here occasionally to use the outside privy before going on another half-hour to the turn-off to El Perico. Today she stopped only to stretch her legs and say hello to Nicanor Gallegos, the owner of the station.

"It's getting cold out there," Larissa said to Nicanor as she entered the station building and moved immediately toward the large wood-burning stove.

"We're expecting a snow storm. Are you going up or down?" Nicanor scratched at a scab on the back of his hand.

"I'm going up. We're breaking camp today." Larissa laid a dollar on the counter and pointed to the small bags of salted peanuts.

Nicanor handed Larissa one of the bags. "You'd better hurry or it's going to snow on you." He laid her change on the counter. "Good thing you have snow tires on your van."

Larissa picked up her money, said good-bye, and got back into her vehicle. By the time she turned off the highway onto the dirt road leading up to the dig site, a light snow had already speckled the ground. She hurried to the top of the mesa and parked next to where Eloy and Marcos were loading the College van. Larissa got out, put on her heavy jacket, and opened her van's backdoor.

"What do you want me to take back?" Larissa asked.

"All of those bags of garbage." Eloy pointed to a number of bulging garbage bags. "And take those two cardboard boxes of junk and the left-over groceries."

Larissa saw an apparently overlooked coil of rope on the ground, so she dropped it into one of the boxes. As she loaded the items into the back of her van, she realized she had not seen José.

"Isn't José García here?" Larissa looked around for the student.

"He's gone looking for Wolf. They'd better hurry up and get back here. The snow is getting heavier." Eloy turned to Marcos and told him to get into the van.

"Why is Aaron Wolf up here?"Larissa was surprised at what Eloy had said.

"I asked him to come help me. He went over to the south side of the mesa where I had found some more man-made ruins. He's been over there several hours." Eloy got into his van.

Just as Larissa closed the back door, José returned to the camp site and quickly reported, "I didn't find Dr. Wolf. He's not over there."

"Well, we can't wait any longer. The snow is already coming down too heavy. We've got to get off this mesa." Eloy motioned for José to hurry.

Larissa quickly spoke up. "Eloy, we can't leave Dr. Wolf up here." She could not believe he would abandon Aaron.

"Relax. The man's an Indian. He'll be all right out here—besides, there's the camper trailer— he can shelter in it." Eloy got into his van. "Don't worry about him— he'll probably make it down to

50

the highway and catch a ride—if not—I'll come back for him." Eloy started his van's engine. "You'd better leave, too, Larissa."

"Eloy, for God's sake! What's wrong with you? Aaron is no different than anyone else. He can die of hypothermia just like we all can." She stood and watched Eloy drive away.

Larissa did not waste any time, but got into her van and drove over to the south side of the mesa. In the areas where she could not drive her vehicle, she parked and got out and searched for Aaron. Not finding him, she drove up and down the snow-covered road which traversed the large mesa top while honking the van's horn every few minutes. This did not help her find Aaron. The storm continued and the snow began piling up. For at least an hour, Larissa drove everywhere she could on top of the mesa.

On the south side, Larissa had noticed an area near a stand of pines where the ground seemed to drop oddly away from the edge of the mesa top. For some reason this drop-off grabbed her attention, so she went back and parked. She got out and looked down a shallow gully. About fifteen feet down she noticed something unnatural, something lumpy under the snow.

Larissa carefully slid down the incline on her buttocks. At the bottom she found Aaron with part of his body lying in a small rock indention filled with water. She quickly wiped the snow from his head and face. He had a large gash on the top of his head.

Aaron tried to talk as he shivered violently. "I'm dizzy. Help me get up." He looked up at Larissa.

She tried to help him onto his feet, but she realized he had an ankle injury and could not stand. Aaron grasped Larissa's arm and groaned, and she suspected he was experiencing a lot of pain.

"Aaron, I'm going to get you out of here. I promise you I will." She helped him lie down again.

Carefully she crawled back up the incline on her hands and knees. Her first thought was to go down to La Zorilla to get Nicanor Gallegos to come back and help her. The round trip to La Zorilla on a good day took at least an hour. Today, with the snow, perhaps she could not get the van back up the steep dirt road leading up to the mesa. There were no options; she would have to get Aaron up to the van by herself.

Opening the van's back door, Larissa emptied the two large cardboard boxes of their contents, and then collapsed the boxes to make a long, flat pad to put under Aaron's body. Carrying the cardboard and a small paring knife, and with the coil of rope over her shoulder, she slowly went back down to where Aaron lay shivering, curled in a fetal position.

She used the small knife to cut a piece of the cardboard and rope with which she stabilized Aaron's ankle. Then she rolled him onto the remaining piece of cardboard, and, with the rope, tied him tightly on it. With the other end of the rope tied around her waist, she crawled back up to the top. She tried to pull Aaron up but he weighed too much for her.

By now, the snow was falling heavily. Larissa turned her van around so that it faced the embankment, and then she tied the rope to the front bumper. Slowly she backed the van about ten feet, got out and looked down. Seeing Aaron almost at the top, she got into the van and backed it slowly until she had Aaron all the way up the incline.

She untied the rope, turned the van around, and backed it to where Aaron lay. She threw the garbage bags out, and then freed Aaron from the cardboard. He looked up at her when she bent over him, and he grabbed her arm and tried to get up. With their combined effort, he got into the back of the van where he lay in a shivering heap. Larissa quickly unrolled her sleeping bag, but she did not want to put him in it with his wet clothing.

She turned the van's heater control to its highest setting and closed the back door. As she took off Aaron's wet boots and socks, she noticed his left ankle appeared extremely swollen. The thought of it being broken crossed her mind. Aaron did not do much to help her, but he did not resist while she removed all his clothing.

As she rolled him over onto the opened sleeping bag, he moaned and mumbled a few incoherent words. Because his feet felt extremely cold, she removed her shoes and socks and tried unsuccessfully to put one of her socks on his swollen left foot. She stabilized his injured ankle again and, in desperation, she took off her fleece-lined jacket and wrapped it around Aaron's feet. Then she quickly zipped him into the sleeping bag.

Because his hair was wet, Larissa took out his braids. Then she removed her flannel shirt and used it to dry his hair as much as she could. With her tee-shirt, she wrapped his head to keep his body warmth from escaping. She spread his wet clothes on the front seat, hoping the heater would help dry them. Aaron continued to shiver and his lips appeared blue. Hypothermia crossed Larissa's mind, and she feared he might die.

Next, she did something she would not have done except for a story her father had told her about his grandmother and her sister having saved a man from dying. Like her great-grandmother had done before her, Larissa took off all her clothing, got into the sleeping bag, and put her warm body up against the naked body of a very cold man.

Larissa tried to warm Aaron the best she could by lying next to him. She briskly rubbed his arms and hands. Finally, she pulled the sleeping bag over their heads and wrapped her arms and legs around his body. It took a while before Aaron finally stopped shivering.

From time to time Larissa got out of the sleeping bag and checked the van's fuel gauge. She knew it would do them no good if she used up all the fuel to keep the van warm. Knowing she had to be able to drive Aaron back to Los Espíritus, she turned off the engine, occasionally running it only long enough to warm the van. She used her damp flannel shirt to cover her body during her time out of the sleeping bag.

Sometime after midnight, Larissa noticed it had almost stopped snowing, but she decided not to start down the snow-covered road in the dark. She turned off the engine, which had been running for about fifteen minutes, climbed back into the sleeping bag, and unsuccessfully tried to fall asleep. Aaron did not rest easily, but tossed and turned and moaned a good deal of the night. He seemed to be aware of her, because he called her name and asked her for water. Several times she coaxed him to swallow aspirins which she had brought with her. When his body finally felt warm and relaxed, she got out of the sleeping bag and put on her clothes.

At daybreak, Larissa decided to try to make it to the highway where she hoped she might get help. Perhaps she could drive all the way to La Zorilla, but her resolve was to get Aaron to the hospital in Los Espíritus.

She got out of the van without her jacket which still enveloped Aaron's feet. There were perhaps ten inches of snow on the ground. Although the cold penetrated Larissa's denim jeans and flannel shirt, she trudged in the deep snow around the van, removing the snow from all of the windows with a small piece of cardboard. The cold air sent sharp pains into her lungs with every breath she took. Then she got back into the van and warmed her cold hands by blowing on them with her warm breath. Only then could she grasp the steering wheel.

The van's tires dug into the snow and gained enough traction to move the van forward to the place where the dirt road started its decent down from the mesa. Negotiating the steep, winding part of the road was harrowing. Using the brakes often, Larissa inched the van down the road. The tires made crunching sounds as they slowly turned through the deep snow. There were times when the tires slipped, and Larissa feared losing control of the vehicle.

When she reached the end of the dirt road, Larissa encountered a thick blanket of snow covering the highway which indicated no vehicles had come through. She drove the van onto the highway and proceeded slowly toward La Zorilla. In some places, the snow had drifted and banked, and she had to increase her speed to move through the drifts. Determining exactly where the edge of the winding road's pavement met the rough, rocky shoulder gave Larissa some trouble. It took about two hours to reach La Zorilla with Aaron moaning a good deal of the way.

When Larissa pulled off the highway in front of Nicanor Gallegos's service station, she turned off the engine and put her head over on the steering wheel for several minutes. Her legs were uncontrollably shaking as she got out of the van and walked over to the door of the station. She found it locked. When she peered through the window, she realized the station was closed. Looking toward the area behind the station building, Larissa noticed smoke coming from the chimney pipe of an old adobe house. She hurried to the house and found Nicanor Gallegos.

He seemed surprised to see her. "How did you get here? The road is closed."

"I just came off of El Perico Mesa, and I have an injured man in my van. I need to get him to a hospital." Larissa's voice broke.

Nicanor motioned for Larissa to come into his warm, one-room house. It smelled of pine smoke and strong coffee. Nicanor's wife looked up for a moment and then continued rolling a flour tortilla. Three young children stared at Larissa with large, brown eyes and unanimated faces. A tiny baby slept in a crib.

"Let me call up to Canyon Springs and see if they're going to send down the snow plow anytime soon. There's no way you can get through to Los Espíritus—the drifts are probably too high at some of the passes." Nicanor picked up the telephone receiver, put it to his ear, and turned a crank on the side of the phone.

Larissa smiled because she had not seen this type of telephone since her childhood when a trunk line into Albuquerque provided the only service for Los Espíritus. She always enjoyed cranking the phone in the cantina to tell the operator what number she wanted. Of course, back then there were only about fifteen telephones in town, all on the same line. Some people listened in to other's conversations a good deal of the time. As far as telephones in La Zorilla, it pleased Larissa to see one, even if it was the old-fashioned kind.

Nicanor hung up the receiver. "You're in luck. The snow plow will be getting down here within the hour. You can follow it to Los Espíritus."

Larissa gave a sigh of relief and said, "Listen, could I buy a cup of coffee from you? And do you have any kind of pain pills? The man in the van needs something." Larissa had no more aspirins to give Aaron, and it would be several hours before they would reach Los Espíritus.

"Delia, pour this lady a cup of coffee," Nicanor said to his wife as he walked over to a cupboard where he took out a bottle with a small amount of whiskey in it. "Give this to the man. It should be enough to take the edge off his pain."

Larissa took the whiskey and pulled a ten dollar bill out from the pocket of her jeans. "And my van needs gasoline." Then thanking Nicanor's wife, Larissa picked up the cup of coffee.

Nicanor put on his heavy fleece-lined jacket. "You don't owe me anything for the coffee and whiskey." He opened the door for Larissa.

While Nicanor filled up the van's fuel tank, Larissa got into the back with Aaron. She held his head up and offered him the whiskey.

He opened his eyes, took a big swallow, and said, "Larissa, help me, please help me."

"Yes, Aaron, I'm helping you. I'll get you to the hospital." She was relieved to see him awake and talking coherently.

"I need to get out." He began trying to unzip the sleeping bag.

"No, Aaron, you can't get out. You're naked and your ankle is too injured." She tried to calm him.

"Damn it, Larissa, I have to get out and pee!" He tried again to unzip the sleeping bag.

Larissa remembered the large coffee can she had taken from one of the cardboard boxes. The can was on the floorboard in front of the passenger seat with some of the other groceries. She got it and emptied the small amount of ground coffee into another container. Then she unzipped the sleeping bag just enough to put the can in for Aaron. She attempted to hold it in place for him.

He looked at her. "Go away," he said.

Larissa continued holding the can. "I will if you'll hold this for yourself. We've still got a long road ahead of us, and you need to be comfortable, so please go ahead and use the can." She let go of the can as he took it from her.

"Don't look," he snapped.

Larissa snorted and said, "You don't have anything I want to look at. And you'd better not pee on my sleeping bag." Larissa turned her head away from him, but only so he would not see her struggling to keep from laughing.

Nicanor finished filling the tank and Larissa thanked him for his help. Then while she savored her cup of lukewarm coffee, she made Aaron drink the rest of the whiskey. He had just finished it when the snow plow came down the highway from the north. Larissa pulled the van in behind the plow and drove to Los Espíritus, getting there by early afternoon without any problems.

After arriving at the small hospital on the edge of town, several attendants took Aaron, still enclosed in Larissa's sleeping bag, into the emergency room. Larissa told the hospital staff what had happened. Someone asked for the name of Aaron's emergency contact person, but because Larissa knew nothing about Aaron's personal business, she suggested they call the history department at the College. Then she went home and washed, dried, and ironed Aaron's clothing. She set his damp boots in front of the fireplace, but they did not dry fast enough to suit her, so she lit the oven and set the boots on the opened oven door.

As soon as she had Aaron's clothes ready, Larissa went back to the hospital. She talked to the same nurse who had been there when she had arrived with Aaron.

"Mr. Wolf will be kept overnight for observation. We sutured his head laceration and have immobilized his ankle. If he has no other injuries, he should be all right. I can't tell you anything else." The nurse gave Larissa the report without smiling.

"Is it possible for me to see him?" Larissa meekly asked.

"No. He's been sedated. He needs to rest." The nurse looked very sternly at Larissa.

"Well, then here are Aaron Wolf's clothes. I took them home and laundered them so he would have something to wear when he leaves the hospital." Larissa held out the large paper bag containing Aaron's boots and clothing.

The nurse frowned, took the bag. "A woman has already brought Mr. Wolf some clothes." Then the nurse gave Larissa a big smile.

Larissa tried to return the smile, but she could not. She wondered about the woman who had brought Aaron his clothing. Larissa said thank you to the nurse, and as she turned to leave, the nurse smiled again at Larissa. Larissa did not smile back, and she did not smile as she drove home. In fact, she would not smile again until she looked into the eyes of Aaron Wolf.

Chapter Five

Eloy Flores seemed to waste no time in confronting Larissa in her office on Thursday morning. He came in without knocking as usual.

"Well, sweetheart, aren't you the big heroine for finding Wolf? And you've already presented a written complaint against me to Ríos. You're a busy little girl, aren't you, *mi amor*?" Eloy did not attempt to move nearer to Larissa.

"Is that all you wanted to tell me, Eloy?" Larissa avoided eye contact. She was irritable and did not want to discuss anything with Eloy, but it pleased her that he kept his distance from her this morning.

"Just so you'll know, Pete Ríos said I had every right to leave Wolf up on the mesa because I had the students' welfare to think of. Besides, Wolf didn't represent the anthropology department or the College." Eloy sat down across the desk from Larissa.

Larissa glared at Eloy. "You're right, but you asked him to go with you to the site to help you. You're his good friend, remember?" Larissa began straightening some papers on her desk. She wanted to get rid of Eloy so she could start her work for the day. She also wanted to find out from someone in the history department about Aaron's condition.

Eloy leaned back in the chair. "Another thing you should know, *mi amor*, is you'd better not have any ideas of trying to get something romantic going with Wolf. He's got no use for a silly, immature woman like you." Eloy leaned farther back and clasped his hands behind his head. "He's already had his heart torn out by a stupid woman."

Larissa dropped a paper from her hand and looked up at Eloy. "What are you talking about?"

"Wolf was engaged to a beautiful woman when I knew him in Oklahoma, and he had expectations of marrying her." Eloy hesitated and sneered at Larissa. "He loved her very much and probably still does."

Larissa shrugged her shoulders. "So, why didn't he marry her?" She wanted to know more about Aaron and the woman without appearing too interested.

"She proved to be unfaithful to him with one of his good friends. I heard Wolf himself caught them in bed together." Eloy laughed. "What a blow to a man's ego. Anyway, I suspect he doesn't trust women anymore. I'm just warning you to stay away from him." Eloy stood up.

Larissa looked away from Eloy. "Well, that's too bad. I'm sorry for him."

Eloy walked to the doorway. "Just keep your hands off of him. He's probably already decided he doesn't even like you." Eloy walked away.

"I bet he does like me," Larissa whispered to herself as she heard Eloy leave the building.

Later in the day, Larissa went to the history department and asked the secretary about Aaron. The secretary reported Aaron had a number of bruises, his ankle had been badly sprained, and he would be staying at home for several days. Larissa felt relief to know Aaron's ankle had not been broken, and he had received no other serious injuries.

* * *

On the following Monday, Larissa noticed Aaron's pickup parked in the faculty lot. All day, as she went about her tasks, she expected him to come to the museum to see her, but he never came. Disappointed, she went home thinking she would go to bed early.

Larissa and Carmelita ate supper together, and afterwards, Larissa stretched out on the sofa and fell asleep. Carmelita had just finished washing the supper dishes and had walked out the back door to go home when someone knocked on the front door. The knocking awakened Larissa, so she arose and went to the door and slowly opened it. There, in front of her, stood Aaron on crutches with a long–stemmed red rose in his right hand. He held the rose out to her.

"Good evening, Larissa. You deserve more than one rose, but I knew I couldn't carry more than one and hang on to the crutches at the same time." He smiled.

Larissa took the rose. "Aaron! Thank you! Come on in and let me look at you." Larissa did not hide the pleasure that seeing him gave her.

He slowly came in on the crutches. A splint enveloped his left ankle. As Aaron walked by, King Carlos roused from his nap on the bear rug.

"Come sit at the dining room table. I think those chairs are higher, and it will be more comfortable for you." Larissa escorted him into the dining room. "And tell me, how is it you can drive your pickup with an injured ankle?"

"It has an automatic transmission. I have more trouble getting into the pickup than I do driving it." He sat down in a chair that Larissa pulled out for him.

"Are you hungry? Do you want a piece of Carmelita's special coconut cream pie?" Larissa walked to the kitchen doorway and waited for Aaron's reply.

He smiled and nodded, so Larissa quickly brought him a big serving of the pie. She also put the rose in a bud vase and placed it in the middle of the dining table.

"I'm glad to see you're on your feet and doing well. I feared you might die of hypothermia. That's why I did what I did, and I hope it didn't upset you." Larissa sat down across the table from Aaron and fixed her eyes on him.

He had a puzzled look on his face. "What did you do?" He took a bite of Carmelita's pie.

"I took your clothes off. They were wet." Larissa looked down at the table.

"No, that didn't upset me." Aaron continued eating the pie.

"Not even when I took off all my clothes and got into the sleeping bag with you?" Larissa looked him squarely in the face.

He did not say anything for a few moments, and then he said very slowly, "I thought I dreamed that."

Larissa took a big breath. "No, Aaron, it really happened, but I want to explain to you why I did it. My father told me years ago about his grandmother and her sister saving a man's life by putting him in their bed between their naked bodies." She hesitated and took another breath. "Their father had found the man nearly dead in a snow bank near their ranch house. I remembered my father's story when I found you so cold and wet."

Aaron looked at Larissa without any expression on his face. "Well, I hope I conducted myself like a gentleman, and do you happen to have any coffee?"

Larissa got up, went into the kitchen, and came back with a cup and the pot of coffee left from supper. She poured some coffee into his cup. When she set the cup down in front of Aaron, he took her hand and kissed the back of it.

Then he looked up at her. "Thank you for rescuing me." He continued holding her hand and looking up at her.

"You're welcome." She slowly pulled her hand away.

She sat down across from him and watched him as he drank his coffee. They did not talk, but just looked at one another. Finally, he held his empty cup out to her, and she poured him more coffee.

Aaron stirred a spoonful of sugar into his coffee and then reached for the canned milk. Larissa watched him in silence.

Finally, Larissa said, "Aaron, I need to tell you something about Eloy and me." She noticed the expression on Aaron's face changed. "He has been inappropriate with me ever since I first came to work at Santa Elena College."

"What has he done?"

"He says things and he gropes me and pats me on the buttocks. I have to be on guard just to have a conversation with him. I can't relax around him, so it's difficult to work with him." She stopped to see if Aaron would say anything.

Aaron frowned. "Do you think you've done anything to cause it?"

"I've done nothing! Why would you ask what I've done to deserve this kind of abuse?"

"Sorry, I just wondered if you and Eloy may have had an affair." Aaron took a taste of his coffee.

"No! I wouldn't have an affair with a married man, and I've never been in any way attracted to Eloy." Larissa slowly shook her head. "Sometimes he just says lewd things to me, but other times, he puts his hands on me. I've asked him to quit bothering me."

"Why don't you report his behavior to your department head?" Aaron gently stirred a little more sugar into his coffee.

"I've done that already. Dr. Ríos has a stack of reports from me. He told me I could possibly get Eloy fired, but Eloy has tenure, so it will take an investigation and a hearing—and even then, it could backfire on me." Larissa stopped talking and looked down at the table.

Aaron quickly said, "I'm sorry about your problem with Eloy."

Larissa looked up. "Please understand that I've mentioned it to you only because you and Eloy are friends, and I don't know what he might say to you about me."

"He's never said anything." Aaron stood up. "Thanks for the coffee and thank Carmelita for the pie."

He fumbled around trying to get his crutches up under him. Larissa helped him put them in place. They walked together into the living room where Larissa stopped, blocking Aaron's way toward the door. She turned and faced him.

Aaron stood between the sofa and the bear rug looking at her. "Thank you again, Larissa, for everything you did for me." Aaron tried to take her hand, but he seemed clumsy with the crutches. He bent over and kissed her lightly on her cheek.

She continued standing in front of him with a slight smile on her face "You're welcome. And tell me, is that the kind of kiss I can always expect from you, either on my hand or on my cheek?"

Aaron chuckled. "Well, I guess so, in light of what you told me when we first met—you said you weren't interested in anything serious because you were too busy with your work. I sure don't want to detract you from your work, Dr. Lozoya."

"What if I should change my mind?" Larissa did not move.

"Then I would kiss you on your lips," he said.

"Good, because I just changed my mind," she said.

He moved his head toward hers and gently touched her lips with his. She still did not move away from him. Then he let one of his crutches fall against the sofa, and he wrapped his free arm around her, drew her to him, and kissed her squarely on her lips. They sat down on the sofa and he pulled her over onto his lap and gave her more of the same kind of kisses.

"I'm glad you changed your mind," he said.

"Me, too," she said.

"And something else." He whispered in her ear, "I lied to you. I didn't dream you were naked in the sleeping bag. I knew you were naked. And even though I was in a lot of pain, you nearly drove me crazy."

Larissa gasped. "Aaron, I'm so sorry. I didn't mean to do anything wrong. Please understand."

"I understand, but next time I may not be a gentleman."

"Next time I may not want you to be."

King Carlos awoke and walked over to Larissa and Aaron. He meowed very loudly, his usual signal for wanting to eat. He meowed again.

"He needs his supper. I guess I'd better go feed him." Larissa stood up and helped Aaron up and onto his crutches, and then she walked with him to the front door.

"I want to come see you again soon." Aaron hesitated at the door.

"You're always welcome. I've already said you can spend all the time you need in the den with my father's old documents and photos." Larissa opened the door for Aaron.

"Yes, I know, but I said I want to come see *you*." He kissed her gently on her lips and walked out.

Larissa closed the door and went to the kitchen with King Carlos following her. She put some of his favorite cat food into his bowl. He walked over to the bowl, smelled the food, and walked out of the kitchen.

"*Pinche gato*," Larissa said, and she turned out the lights and went to bed.

Chapter Six

The day had turned cold and *piñon* smoke from many chimneys spread over Los Espíritus. It was Friday afternoon and few people were on campus. Larissa enjoyed the solitude and had worked most of the day on display cases. Two of the dioramas were completely finished, and she had begun to think the project might be completed on time. She sat down on the settee in her office to rest a few minutes and to decide if she should stay a few more hours working on the text for some of the display case items.

"Are you there, *mi amor?*" Eloy Flores opened the door, stepped into Larissa's office, and closed the door behind him.

As Eloy stood leering at her, Larissa contemplated moving to her desk to be closer to the telephone. However, that would put her closer to Eloy so she decided not to move.

Larissa glared at Eloy. "I'm tired of telling you to quit saying *mi amor.* I'm not your love."

Eloy quickly rushed to the settee, grabbed Larissa by the upper arms, and pulled her up against him. She tried to pull away, but he held her too tightly. Eloy attempted to kiss Larissa on her lips as she squirmed and turned her head from side to side. When he tried to push her down onto the settee, she kneed him in the crotch, and he quickly turned her loose.

Larissa said nothing but took a seat on the settee and watched as her colleague bent over, grabbed his crotch with both hands, and exited her office. Larissa quickly arose and went to her desk. She dialed the telephone number of Pete Ríos's office. He did not answer. Thinking he may have already left campus, she dialed his home number. Pete Ríos answered.

"Dr. Ríos, this is Larissa. Eloy Flores just came into my office and inappropriately put his hands on me. He tried to kiss me and push me down onto the settee. I've already given you a number of incident reports concerning Dr. Flores's inappropriate behavior toward me, and now this has happened."

"Well, Larissa, were you provocative with him?" Pete Ríos sounded snappish and condescending.

"No. I was not."

"Well, are you wearing something sexy or revealing?"

"No. I'm wearing baggy jeans and a big sweater."

"Did you say something to him to make him think you were sexually interested in him?"

"Dr. Ríos, I assure you that I say as little as possible to Eloy. In fact, I avoid him, and why would I be interested in a middle-aged married man?" Pete Ríos's suggestions angered Larissa. "Furthermore, my clothing is more modest than most of the females on this campus, and you know that's true."

"If you didn't cause him to do it, Larissa, then I don't know what's gotten into him." Pete Ríos paused. "That darned Eloy."

Larissa thought Pete Ríos did not sound very concerned. In fact, she was almost sure she heard him chuckle.

Larissa took a deep breath. "If you don't do something about this, I'm going to the dean and even to the president of the College if I have to!" Larissa's anger caused her voice to be louder than normal. She stopped and waited for Pete Ríos's reply.

He cleared his throat. "Well, Larissa, this sounds serious. I'll talk to Eloy first thing Monday morning." He hesitated. "And, Larissa, don't do anything until I get back to you."

To Larissa, Pete Ríos seemed to be a little more concerned, but not much. She hung up the telephone and shuddered. This entire business with Eloy made her angry and disgusted. He had become a constant source of irritation, and she found him nearly impossible to work with because of his groping and inappropriate innuendos. She hated how he had left Aaron on the mesa in the snow storm, and now this.

Larissa did not want any more of Eloy's abuse. Of course, she could write another incident report and give it to Pete Ríos, but the reports were beginning to pile up. Reporting to Pete Ríos seemed highly ineffective, so she decided to do something else. She called the Los Espíritus police station. Explaining the nature of the incident, she asked to have someone come to her office.

Larissa had hoped the police department would provide a woman to investigate the complaint. However, she seriously doubted there were any women employed by the department, and, of course, a male officer responded. His business with Larissa did not take much time, and he wrote down the information without making any unnecessary comments. He did ask what she had done or said just before Eloy grabbed her. Larissa replied she did not remember doing anything, but she had told Eloy not to call her his love.

Then the officer asked, "Are you having or have you had a sexual affair with Eloy Flores?"

"No, and I've never had a sexual affair with anybody, not now, not ever," Larissa said emphatically, thinking the officer probably did not believe her.

When the officer completed the interview, he told Larissa someone might contact her for further information. He left and Larissa locked the building and walked home in the chill of the late afternoon.

When she arrived home, she found Carmelita in the kitchen putting a pie in the refrigerator.

"Look, *muchacha*, I made this coconut cream pie for your *novio*," Carmelita said and flashed a sly little smile to Larissa.

"You made it for whom?" Larissa had not paid much attention to what Carmelita had just said to her because her thoughts were on the burial robes she needed to clean.

"I made it for your sweetheart. It's from one of my best recipes, and it's coconut, the kind he likes." Carmelita smiled and rubbed her hands together.

Larissa had forgotten about Aaron's plans to come over to work on the materials in the file drawer. He usually came three or four nights a week to her house, but he did not always come to work. Sometimes they went for walks, occasionally they visited with Mimi at the cantina, and sometimes they attended free concerts at the College. Because Larissa had not forgotten about the financial obligations which Aaron had mentioned to her when they first met, she made certain not to put any monetary demands on him. They never went out for dinner and seldom went to movies. Usually, during an evening of working on their various projects, Larissa would serve Aaron a light supper and a piece of Carmelita's cream pie.

"Oh, my goodness, yes the pie." Larissa walked over to the older woman and bent over and hugged her. "Thank you so much, Carmelita. I had forgotten about Aaron coming tonight. I had my mind on a chore I have to do."

After Carmelita had gone home, Larissa laid a white bed sheet over the dining room table. Cleaning the burial robes would be a tedious and time-consuming project, and Larissa did not look forward to it. She put on a pair of cotton gloves and carefully removed the two burial robes from the case in her father's den and placed them on the sheet on the dining table. With a soft bristle brush, she began cleaning the large robe. The garment appeared old and very delicate, and she worried she might cause damage to it.

Larissa had just finished removing the dust from the robe when Aaron arrived. The time had passed quickly and Larissa had not stopped the work to put on a fresh pot of coffee. Oh, well, she did not care, the robes were more important. Of course, it delighted her to see Aaron as usual, and she enjoyed the quick hug he gave her after she opened the front door for him. She led him into the dining room.

"I see you are serious about donating the burial robes to the museum," he said.

"Of course I am, but I just wish I knew more about them." She looked down at the beautiful garments and slowly shook her head. "I can't identify all of the feathers."

"Well, for sure the large robe is made of turkey feathers," said Aaron. "But the small one has some other type of feather in addition to turkey. I'm not certain what it is."

Larissa sat down and sighed. "I've already talked to Ted McNorton in Santa Fe. I described the robes to him, and he said to send him some photos. He thinks he can help me as to their origins, but he needs to see the type of textile and weave."

Aaron looked down at the robes and shook his head. "I just don't understand how your father could rob graves."

"You don't know that my father robbed any graves." Larissa frowned at Aaron. "Who knows how my father got these? I would guess he probably gave someone whiskey or wine for them, something he did a lot, especially for jewelry and blankets."

"Sounds like a purveyor of fire water," Aaron said and looked away from her.

"For goodness sakes, Aaron, you know he owned a cantina. People came in wanting a beer or a bottle of wine, and if they didn't have money, my father would trade for something. And not just from the natives, but from anybody. He took in a lot of junk, too. It wasn't often priceless Native American artifacts."

Larissa suspected Aaron found this a delicate subject, and she did not want to discuss it anymore. Nor should he be told tonight about the contents of the two burlap bags she kept out in the apartment.

Aaron went back to the den to continue his work with the photos and documents, and Larissa began cleaning the small robe on the dining table. They worked silently for at least two hours before Larissa decided she needed to stop. She put on a pot of coffee and got the pie out of the refrigerator.

She walked into the den. "Do you want some coconut cream pie? Carmelita made one for you."

He looked up from his work. "Yes, and I'd like some coffee, too. It's getting a little cold in here." He put away the materials and turned out the den light.

She took him to the kitchen and cut the pie and poured him a cup of coffee. He thanked her and told her to thank Carmelita.

"And give her a kiss from me, too," he added as he sat down at the kitchen table.

"I will, but you have to give me the kiss first, and then I'll give it to her." Larissa looked at Aaron and slightly smiled.

"I'll give you as many kisses as you want, only some of them you can't give to Carmelita. They are special and only for you." Aaron took a piece of pie from Larissa.

King Carlos came into the kitchen and walked to his empty food bowl and meowed loudly. Larissa picked up the almost-empty bag of cat food and poured the remainder of the contents into the bowl. She had forgotten to buy a new bag, so she put the left-over tuna fish salad from her lunch into the cat's bowl. King Carlos gulped the tuna down quickly and meowed for more.

"No, sir, no more tuna fish tonight," Larissa said to King Carlos. "Eat your dried cat food."

When they had finished in the kitchen, Larissa told Aaron she would put the robes away for the night because she was too tired to continue with the tedious work. She was also too mentally exhausted to tell Aaron about the incident with Eloy and the police report. If she mentioned it to him, he would probably ask her questions, especially about her interactions with Eloy.

"Are you sure you don't want me to help you work on the small robe?" Aaron asked.

Larissa looked deeply into his eyes. "No, there's something else I'd rather be doing with you than cleaning artifacts."

"What would you rather being doing?" He raised his eyebrows.

"I'd rather be making love to you." She turned and took her black silk shawl from the back of the chair and put it over her shoulders.

"Do you mean having sex?" he asked.

"I didn't say anything about having sex. I said making love to you." She shivered and tied the shawl around her shoulders.

"Larissa, how do you make love without having sex?" He reached over and took her hand from under her shawl.

"I'll show you. But first, put some more wood on the fire and take off your boots."

While Aaron tended to the fire in the living room, Larissa gently folded clean sheets around the two burial robes and placed them in the bottom drawer of the buffet near the dining room table. A tiny feather fell from the small robe and floated to the floor under the table. Larissa did not notice it.

After turning off most of the lights, Larissa brought pillows and a large wool blanket into the living room. She placed these on the bear rug while Aaron, seated on the sofa, removed his boots. King Carlos roused from his sleep in front of the fireplace, stood up and yawned, and walked into the dining room.

Larissa and Aaron lay down on the bear rug under the wool blanket. Aaron turned toward Larissa and pulled her to him and kissed her.

"Aaron, lie on your back and be still. I said I'm going to make love to you."

He pulled her over on top of him and held her tightly against him. She pressed her lips gently against his neck.

In the dining room, King Carlos walked back and forth in front of the bottom drawer of the buffet. While he sniffed along where the drawer did not quite meet the frame, Larissa closed her eyes

81

and enjoyed the fragrances of musk and bay rum on Aaron's skin. She placed her legs along the outside of Aaron's body and sat up, straddling him. He pulled her down on his chest and held her against him. She felt his large silver belt buckle as he pushed it against her belly. He pulled her even tighter to him.

King Carlos apparently had finished sniffing along the drawer which held the feather burial robes because he had turned his attention to something he found under the dining table. Meanwhile, Larissa tasted Aaron's lips and noticed a slight scent of mint and garlic which she thoroughly relished.

While Larissa found pleasure in the scent of bay rum in Aaron's hair, King Carlos batted a small down feather with his paw. Then he sniffed at the feather. Larissa had no awareness of King Carlos because she knew only that Aaron's arms were now around her and pulling her tightly down on him. When Aaron's belt buckle dug into the top of Larissa's pubic bone, she moaned. At the same time, King Carlos licked the feather and it went into his mouth. He gagged. Larissa did not hear this because she and Aaron were breathing heavily.

King Carlos gagged again. Then he ran into the living room and vomited in three places on the bear rug. Larissa heard this and smelled the vomit. It had an intense odor of tuna fish. She jumped up and turned on the light.

"My heavens, King Carlos, look what you've done to Brother Bear." Larissa hurried to the kitchen to get paper towels, warm soapy water, and a sponge to clean the bear's fur.

Aaron got up and moved to the sofa. As Larissa wiped up the mess from the bear rug, Aaron put on his boots.

Aaron looked at King Carlos. "I'll never forgive you, you crazy cat." Aaron zipped up his jacket. "And, Larissa, I enjoyed you making love to me, even though there was no sex involved."

Larissa, who had already begun washing the bear fur, looked up at Aaron. "Oh, yes there was sex." She frowned. "Your silver belt buckle had sex with my pubic bone, and it was painful."

"I'm sorry, I didn't know it hurt you," he said.

"Next time take off your belt," she said as she continued cleaning Brother Bear.

"Next time I'll take off my pants," he said.

"Good night, Aaron. Go home." Larissa stood up and smiled at Aaron.

He kissed her on her cheek, "Good night, Larissa, and thank you for the pie and coffee." He kissed her on her lips, and then whispered in her ear, "And my belt buckle thanks you."

He opened the door and walked out. Larissa closed and locked the door and turned out the lights. Then she took King Carlos and lay down with him on the sofa.

"King Carlos, my dear cat, I think I'm madly in love with Aaron Wolf."

She and King Carlos slept on the sofa all night while Brother Bear's fur dried in the warmth from the fireplace.

Chapter Seven

"Are you sure you want me to put more *ajo* in this *caldo*?" Carmelita asked as she held several crushed cloves of garlic above the pot of stew.

"Yes. I already told you he eats lots of garlic," Larissa replied.

Carmelita raised her eyebrows. "*Madre de Dios*, how do you know he does?" She dropped the garlic into the pot.

"Because I've smelled it on his breath, and I've tasted it in his mouth." Larissa quickly stuck her tongue out at Carmelita and then laughed.

"*¡Ay, que muchacha sin vergüenza¡* Are you not ashamed of yourself? Don't tell me you've already gone that far with him?" Carmelita stirred the *caldo*, laid the spoon down, and turned to face Larissa.

"Yes, I've gone that far. He kisses me and I kiss him. I like the taste of his kisses and the smell of his breath, and I'm not ashamed to say so." Larissa reached out her hand and patted Carmelita on her cheek. She dearly loved this little woman.

"*Bueno*, don't feed him too much of my special *caldo* and coconut cream pie tonight, or he won't want to kiss you."

Larissa quickly cut in, "What do you mean? Carmelita, you better not have put any of your special herbs in that caldo."

"Don't worry about that. I just meant that he'll be so full he'll want to go home and go to bed." Carmelita smiled and turned away from Larissa.

"And tell me, my dear Carmelita, what if he gets too sleepy and wants to go to bed here?" Larissa laughed.

Carmelita scowled. "*¡Ay, Dios mío!* I'm coming here early in the morning to clean up this dirty kitchen. I'm sure you'll leave it for me to do." The elderly woman narrowed her eyes and pointed her finger at Larissa. "And I'd better not find any man sleeping in your bed." Carmelita turned away from Larissa and smiled.

"You won't find anyone in my bed. And don't you dare come here tomorrow morning. It's Saturday and I want to sleep late. I'll clean the kitchen myself." Larissa moved to the stove, picked up the large wooden spoon, added her own special ingredient, and stirred the chicken *caldo*.

After Carmelita had gone home, Larissa cleaned King Carlos's litter box. She then bathed and put on a pair of thin silky slacks and a matching blouse. The blouse seemed rather long, so she pulled up the tails and tied them in a knot between her breasts. She made one last pass around the dining table, putting things in order. Aaron would be arriving soon and Larissa wanted everything to look nice and especially herself. Then she sat down to wait for him. However, she could not relax because she felt an uncertainty. It was almost as if she was waiting for something unexpected to happen.

Aaron arrived a little late, but Larissa did not question him. They did not talk much while they ate. Larissa found the *caldo* more delicious than she had expected and had a second helping of it. Aaron liked the caldo so well that he twice asked for more.

"The *caldo* was good," Aaron said but he did not mention the garlic which Larissa thought might be a little too strong for him. He also said, "I like the pajamas you're wearing."

While Aaron ate a big piece of Carmelita's coconut cream pie, Larissa explained to him the differences between sleepwear and lounging wear. He apologized and said he hoped he had not offended her. He also said, "I like the way you look tonight in whatever it is you're wearing."

After they had finished eating, Larissa cleaned off the table, dumped the dishes in the sink while promising herself she'd get up early in the morning to wash them. After locking the back door, she turned off all the lights in the house except for the lamp on the table next to the sofa. Aaron had already added a chunk of *piñon* wood to the fireplace and stood watching it as it began to burn. King Carlos stretched out on Brother Bear and swished his tail back and forth while Larissa walked over to Aaron and took his hand.

"Come sit on the sofa. I want to talk to you." She led Aaron to the sofa. "And take off your belt. That big buckle always hurts me."

Aaron quickly unhooked the silver Navajo buckle and slipped the wide leather belt out of the loops of his jeans. He laid the belt on the end of the sofa and sat down, pulling Larissa down beside him. He softly kissed her cheeks, then her forehead, and finally her lips.

Larissa removed her shoes and turned her entire body toward Aaron. With her face just a few inches from his, she could detect the fragrances of musk, bay rum, and garlic. Aaron put his arms around Larissa and pulled her tightly to his body.

"Aaron, listen to me. I have something I want to ask you." Larissa caressed his face with her hands and asked, "Do you think we could have a love affair?"

She felt him loosen his hold on her, and she thought she had made a mistake by asking the question.

With a puzzled look on his face, Aaron said, "I thought that's what we are having."

She placed her cheek against his and took a deep breath. "I don't think we're having a love affair, at least not totally." Then she whispered in his ear, "There are things happening to me, and it frightens me because I've never felt this way before."

"What are you feeling?"

Larissa hesitated a moment. "Well, there are things I want you to do to me."

"What things do you want me to do?" He yawned, put his arms around her again, and pulled her tightly to him and kissed her neck.

"I shouldn't have to tell you. You know what I'm talking about." Her breathing became shallow and rapid.

"Are you telling me you want us to have sex?" he asked.

She pulled away from him and stood up. "I think sex is just one part of a love affair. I'm ready for the entire affair if you are."

"I've just been waiting for you," he said and yawned again.

"Aaron, please understand I want more from you than just a casual sexual affair." She stood looking down at him.

"Tell me what you want." He reached out and took her hand.

"There must be more than just a physical relationship. Of course I want intimacy, but I also need your friendship, your companionship, and your loyalty."

He slowly stood up and took her into his arms. "I've already been giving you that," he whispered and gently moved his lips across her cheek.

Releasing his hold on Larissa, Aaron sat down on the sofa and removed his boots and then his shirt. He arose from the sofa and moved toward her. "Lie down on the bear rug."

"Okay, but let me get pillows and a blanket."

When Larissa returned she found King Carlos curled up asleep in the middle of Brother Bear. She gently moved her cat to the edge of the rug. He stretched and looked up at Larissa, then curled up and went back to sleep.

Larissa lay on her back, looking up at the firelight dancing on the familiar pattern of the ceiling. With Aaron lying beside her, the feeling of something long anticipated swept over her. He pulled her over against his bare chest and kissed her on the side of her neck. She felt the starched denim of his jeans along the side of her leg.

Then he laid Larissa on her back and pulled all of her hair out from behind her neck and spread it out like a corona around her head. Taking a handful of her long hair, he brought it to his face, nuzzling it and smelling it. Then he kissed her longer and deeper than he ever had before.

Larissa took a few moments to catch her breath then she took his braids, one in each hand. "Aaron, take your hair out for me."

He took the bands from his braids and, with his hands, shook out his hair. Larissa thought of the day in the snow storm when she had dried his hair with her flannel shirt. She had run her fingers though his long black hair hoping someday she would do it again. Now, she caressed his hair and buried her face in it, smelling the faint scent of bay rum. She had never felt this close to another person in all her life.

Larissa suddenly sat up. "Aaron, wait. Before this goes any farther, there's something I should have already told you." She put her mouth to his ear and whispered, "I've waited a long time for the right man, and I've chosen you." She hesitated, took a breath and let it slowly out and said, "And right now—right now—I'm feeling a little dizzy."

He looked up at her. "Well, I'm feeling a little disoriented myself—almost like I've been drugged. Let's just lie here and relax a minute."

Aaron pulled Larissa over onto his chest where she lay listening to his heart beating. She felt a slight tingling which surged through her, and she had the sensation of sinking into Aaron's body. Down, down she sank, lower and lower, down through Aaron and down through the bear rug. The sinking sensation ceased when she felt as if their spirits had united, hers and Aaron's with the spirit of Brother Bear. A feeling of contentedness and well-being came over her, and she felt totally relaxed.

A loud pop caused Larissa's body to jerk, and she opened her eyes. She had been asleep lying on Aaron's chest. She raised her head and looked at the fireplace just in time to see a shower of sparks being sucked up the chimney. A frightened King Carlos loudly meowed and moved toward Larissa.

Aaron gently rolled Larissa onto her back. "That woke me up. I think the log exploded and a piece of it fell too close to the screen." Aaron stood up. "I'll fix it and add another log."

Larissa arose, straightened the pillows, pulled back the blanket, and lay down on the bear rug. Aaron turned and looked down at her. She yawned, smiled, and gestured for him to join her under the blanket. All three, Aaron, Larissa, and King Carlos quickly fell asleep, and Brother Bear, who never slept, kept vigilance all through the night.

***

Larissa did not get up early the next morning to wash the dishes as she had planned. If she had, she might have seen Carmelita walking slowly up the driveway to the back gate. She might have also seen Carmelita stop and look at the pickup truck sitting in the driveway at the back of the house. Larissa probably would have seen Carmelita smile, turn, and walk back down the driveway and out into the street. However, Larissa did not see any of this because she and Aaron and King Carlos were sound asleep, huddled together under the wool blanket on top of Brother Bear.

Chapter Eight

When Larissa awoke, she realized she was under the wool blanket on top of the bear rug. She turned over and saw Aaron sleeping beside her. Smiling, she put her hand on Aaron's shoulder and gently shook him. Aaron arose and, without speaking, got ready to leave. Larissa sat up and watched him put on his shirt and boots.

Before he finished, she stood up and said, "I'll always remember the things you did to me last night."

He took her in his arms and held her while he whispered, "Well, we didn't do very much but sleep. But I'll be back tonight and we can finish what we started."

He released her and turned to leave. She reached down and pulled the blanket up and wrapped it around her body. King Carlos stood up and stretched, looked at Larissa, and then at Aaron. Larissa walked with Aaron to the back door without noticing her cat following just behind her. King Carlos ran out into the courtyard when Aaron opened the door. When Aaron went through the courtyard gate, King Carlos dashed out and ran down the driveway.

"My goodness, King Carlos, get back in here!" Larissa yelled at the cat.

Aaron hurried to retrieve King Carlos, but the cat ran around to the front of the house. Larissa pulled the blanket tighter around her and ran barefoot toward Aaron.

"I don't see him," Aaron said. "And you need to go back into the house before someone sees you in your pajamas."

Larissa stood her ground. "No. I have to find him. And these aren't pajamas."

Aaron frowned at her. "That cat knows where he belongs, and he knows who wants him. You'll see, he'll come back to you," Aaron's frown turned into a smile. "Just like I'm coming back to you tonight."

"Aaron, I'm afraid for King Carlos. He doesn't have testicles or front claws, so he can't defend himself." Larissa worried about the safety of her altered cat.

"Well, no wonder he's trying to get away from you. He's afraid you may cut off something else." Aaron walked to his pickup mumbling about animal mutilation and tampering with nature.

Larissa followed him. He got into his pickup and backed out leaving Larissa standing in the driveway staring at him. She put her arm out of the blanket and waved at Aaron, but he did not acknowledge it. Before she went into the house, she propped the gate open so King Carlos could get in when he returned. Then she took a quick shower, all the time worrying about King Carlos being attacked by vicious dogs or mean tom cats. She dressed quickly with the intentions of getting her van out of the garage, so she could drive up and down the streets looking for her wayward cat. When she went to make sure the front door was locked, she heard a meow. She opened the door and King Carlos walked into the house. He ran straight to the kitchen and sat down by his food bowl.

"No, you naughty cat, I won't reward you for running away. You can go without food for a while, at least until I finish washing the dishes."

Larissa blamed King Carlos's behavior for Aaron seeming a little upset when he left. With King Carlos back in the house, Larissa began thinking about Aaron and what he had said the night before about finishing what they had started. She wondered what would really happen when he returned. The more she thought about this, the more she became anxious and wanted to talk to Mimi.

***

Larissa arrived at the cantina too early to find the establishment open. She knocked loudly and Braulio opened the big carved door.

He seemed surprised to see her. "*Mi reina,* is anything wrong?"

"Nothing's wrong. I just need to be with you and Mimi today." Larissa walked over to one of the tables and sat down. "Is Mimi up yet? I didn't go around to the back because I thought she might still be asleep."

Before Braulio could answer, Mimi came into the cantina. The orange-colored, chenille robe she wore clashed terribly with her red hair. Her face appeared immaculately made up as usual.

Walking up to Larissa, Mimi put her hand on the younger woman's shoulder. "I can tell there's something going on with you, so don't give me any nonsense."

Larissa looked down. "I don't know what it is, but I just don't think I'm the same woman I was yesterday." She looked up at Mimi and grinned.

"Well, well. Did you finally have sex?" Mimi bluntly asked.

"No, not at all. We both fell asleep, but before that . . . well, the things he did to me, and the way I felt. It was weird."

"Do you want to tell me about it?" Mimi sat down in the chair across from Larissa.

"Yes, I do, but . . ." Larissa looked over at Braulio who busied himself with cleaning the back bar.

"Braulio, would you please go pick up the mail? You can finish the cleaning later," Mimi said to the big man who seemed not to be paying much attention to the two women.

After Braulio left, Larissa told Mimi what had occurred the night before.

"Are you in love with him?" Mimi asked.

"I certainly think I am, although it may just be lust and infatuation. You explained those feelings to me when I was a teenager." Larissa hesitated and then sighed loudly. "But, Mimi, I've never felt this way about a man before in my life." Larissa lowered her voice and said, "Even if we never have sex, I still want to be with him. I really care about this man."

"Well, I think he must be in love with you or else he's crazy. Has he said anything about love?"

"No, he hasn't said he loves me, but he says he enjoys being with me." Larissa slowly shook her head. "And he spends a lot of time with me."

Mimi laughed. "Some men just don't like to verbalize commitments and love is a big commitment. Of course, some men say they love you and don't mean it." Mimi hesitated and held up her finger. "Those are the ones you need to be leery of." Mimi reached over and patted Larissa's hand. "But I still think your man is showing he's in love with you or in the process of falling in love."

Larissa sat back in the chair and smiled. She said nothing but sat thinking about what most surely would happen between her and Aaron when he returned to her house that night.

Mimi got up from the table. "I have to get dressed. What are you going to do?"

"Can I just sit here for the rest of the day? I hope I won't be too nervous to go home tonight."

"What are you afraid of?" Mimi sounded a little concerned.

"I really don't know. I have a strange feeling and I just don't want to be alone right now."

Mimi patted Larissa on the shoulder. "It's getting late. I have to get dressed."

While Mimi went about her own business, Larissa sat drinking ginger ale and listening to her favorite songs on the Wurlitzer. After she had played *Tú Solo Tú* about ten times, Mimi, who was now working behind the bar, finally spoke up.

"Larissa, if you don't quit playing that Mexican love song over and over, I'm going to unplug the juke box. It's driving me crazy!"

At noon Braulio went to a nearby café and brought salads back for Larissa and Mimi and a plate of fried chicken for himself. During the afternoon, Larissa did not talk much. She just sat and thought about many things, but mostly about Aaron.

Several patrons came into the cantina who had known Larissa all of her life, and they stopped to chat with her. Trixie Trujillo also came in. She wore a very short red skirt and a tight-fitting, low-necked blouse. Her face, with heavy make-up, appeared garish, and her dried, bleached hair, being so thickly backcombed, resembled a small stack of hay. Trixie did not address Braulio or Larissa, but went straight into the women's restroom.

"Hey, I thought she was living in Colorado." Larissa frowned. "Does she come in here often?" Larissa asked Braulio who had not even looked up when Trixie walked through the room.

"She usually just wants to use the facilities," Braulio quietly said.

Larissa wrinkled her nose. "Is she still working the plaza?" She had known Trixie since grade school and had never liked her, but had forgotten why. Larissa now had found a new reason to dislike Trixie.

"Yes, she and several others hang around the plaza at night, but I don't let them come in here to negotiate any business."

"Good. And I don't like the way Trixie dresses. And what happened to her beautiful brown hair. Just look what she's done to it—all that peroxide. She looks like a prostitute," Larissa said and then laughed at her own humor.

Trixie came out of the restroom and headed for the door. "Thanks, Braulio." She stopped and sneered at Larissa. "Good-bye, Larissa." Then she snorted and quickly walked out of the cantina.

After Trixie left, Mimi sat down at the table with Larissa.

"Just think about this, Larissa. Love affairs are great, and they make you feel so good about yourself." Mimi hesitated, and then slowly shook her head. "But sometimes you can ruin a love affair by getting married."

Larissa frowned. "Is that what you did?"

"Yes, with Hiram. But, of course, not with your father." Mimi patted Larissa on the hand.

"Mimi, tell me the truth, why didn't you and my father ever get married? I know you were lovers."

"He never asked me, although I think if I had pushed it, he would have married me." Mimi batted at a fly buzzing around her head. "Truthfully, Larissa, he never got over his love for your mother. His anger over her death nearly killed him."

"Did he blame me for her death? I've often wondered because she died from giving birth to me."

"No, he never seemed to blame anyone." Mimi turned toward Braulio as he handed her the fly swatter. "Because your father became so angry about your mother's death, he got rid of everything belonging to her, even her photos. I guess he couldn't bear to see anything which reminded him of her. He seemed angry at her for dying." Mimi swatted a fly on the table and brushed it to the floor. "He kept you, of course, and Carmelita to take care of you. You two were the only reminders of your mother."

"What about the silver mirror, brush, and comb on my dresser? Those were hers."

"Carmelita hid those from your father. She wanted to keep something for you." Mimi stood up. "You look just like Lourdes. You know that, don't you?"

"Yes, I know I look like my mother. You've told me many times. But my father hardly ever mentioned my mother to me. How odd." Larissa shook her head and looked down because talking about this made her feel sad. Being close to Mimi and Carmelita, two women who had known her mother, gave Larissa the only sense of connection she had ever had with the woman who had given birth to her.

Later in the afternoon as Larissa sat alone listening to love songs on the juke box, Braulio spoke up. "I hope you haven't left any windows open at your house. There's a warning on the radio that a bad thunderstorm is coming."

Hearing this, Larissa went to the doorway. The day had become cloudy and dark, and the sky toward the southeast looked black.

"I guess I'd better go home before the rain gets here," Larissa said and waved good-bye to Braulio and Mimi.

If Larissa had not left La Llorona Cantina and Dance Hall earlier than she had planned, she would have seen a man in a black suit and a wide-brimmed hat walk through the cantina's front entrance and approach Braulio. She would have heard what the man said, and she would have noticed the man showing Braulio a photograph of a woman. Certainly she would have seen Braulio take the photo, bring it closer to his eyes, and then shake his head. And if Larissa had had the opportunity to see the photo, she most certainly would have recognized the woman. But Larissa was busy driving her van faster than the speed limit and loudly singing her favorite Mexican love song.

Chapter Nine

Upon arriving home, Larissa straightened the living room and put fresh sheets on her bed. She heated some leftovers and ate very little because she did not have much appetite. From time to time she looked out the windows, but the storm seemed far away. She ran water in the bathtub and got out her silky lounging pajamas. Then she relaxed for a long time in the tub. At seven o'clock, Larissa lay down on the couch, and without intending to do so, she fell asleep. About nine o'clock, Aaron's knocking on the glass window of the kitchen door awakened her.

"I knocked and knocked on the front door. What happened to you?" Aaron said as he came into the kitchen.

Larissa, a little dazed from the deep sleep from which she had just been awakened, said, "I'm sorry, I fell asleep, and I didn't hear you until you knocked on the glass."

"There's a thunderstorm coming." Aaron pointed toward the back of the house just as lightning lit up the entire courtyard, and a loud clap of thunder startled Larissa.

King Carlos, having followed Larissa into the kitchen, also seemed to have been frightened by the loud noise. He ran to the dining room and hid under the table.

"Let's get away from the door," Larissa said and took Aaron's hand and led him to the living room just as another bolt of lightning hit nearby.

The lights in the house suddenly went out. Larissa grabbed Aaron's arm. They could see lightning flashes through all of the living room windows.

"Hurry, we should go into the den because there aren't any windows in there," said Larissa.

With the frequent flashes of lightning giving them enough light by which to see, she and Aaron went back through the dining room and to the kitchen where Larissa found Carmelita's tall votive candle with the decal of *Nuestra Señora de Guadalupe* on it. Larissa lit the candle, and she and Aaron went into the den and shut the door behind them. They could not see the lightning, but they heard the loud, rolling thunder which caused the window panes in the other parts of the house to rattle.

Larissa led Aaron over to the large four-poster bed and set the candle on a bedside table. "This bed has a feather mattress. Did you know feather beds are the safest place to be when a lightning bolt strikes?"

"I've never heard that, but I'm willing to test the hypothesis with you," Aaron replied and pulled Larissa onto the bed with him.

Larissa felt the wonderful softness of the feathers envelop her. Then she felt Aaron's arms around her and he pulled her toward him. He moved his lips across her face and down to her neck.

Aaron raised his head, looked down at her, and quietly said, "I've thought all day about you." He tenderly touched her lips with his.

"I've thought about you, too, and I think we need to proceed slowly," Larissa replied.

While Larissa was kissing Aaron all over his face, King Carlos, having come out from under the dining room table, pawed at the den door. He next began meowing loudly, but Larissa did not hear him because she only heard her own heavy breathing. King Carlos left the den door and went to the hall bathroom to his litter box and did something he had never done before. Perhaps he did it on purpose, or perhaps he just lacked the keen eyesight most cats have in the dark. Whatever the cause, he stepped on the edge of the litter box and turned it over, dumping out most of the litter. Then he made a stinky mess on the floor.

Larissa did not know any of this because she was concentrating her efforts on Aaron. She found what he was doing to her so thoroughly enjoyable that she did not hear the rain loudly pelting the window panes throughout the house. The noise of the rain must have frightened King Carlos because he ran to Larissa's empty bedroom and jumped upon the dresser, knocking everything onto the floor. He quickly jumped down and hid under the bed.

Larissa did not know what her cat had done, but she did know she was experiencing something unique. At that point a loud crash of thunder shook the house so hard that Larissa thought she felt the bed trembling. She slowly raised her head and looked at Aaron. In the flickering light from Carmelita's votive candle, Larissa could see a puzzled look on his face.

105

"Are you okay?" she asked. "That one sounded like it could have caused an earthquake."

"Yes, I'm okay, but what about you?

"I'm fine," she responded. "In fact, I think I'm better than I've ever been." She smiled and snuggled up against Aaron's body.

King Carlos came out from under the bed in Larissa's bedroom when the heavy rain stopped. He returned to the den door and meowed and pawed the door and meowed some more. Larissa did not hear this as she could hear only Aaron whispering in her ear how much he enjoyed being with her. He also called her his sweetheart. Larissa delighted in hearing his words. Aaron told her he liked her hair, her eyes, her nose, and her lips. She whispered to Aaron that she thought him kind and gentle and the only man in the world she wanted to have in bed beside her.

King Carlos continued meowing at the den door. When Larissa did not let him in, he went into the kitchen and jumped into the sink and licked the food left on a plate. When he had finished, he knocked an empty juice glass off the counter, and it fell to the floor and shattered. The startled cat jumped down onto a small piece of broken glass, cutting the pad of his right front paw.

King Carlos ran back into Larissa's bedroom where he jumped onto her bed and began licking his wound. Of course, he had made a bloody trail on the floor from the kitchen, through the dining room, down the hall, and then all over the white satin spread on Larissa's bed.

When his paw quit bleeding he went back into the kitchen where he leapt onto the stove and sniffed around. He smelled the covered container of bacon grease and tried to open it. He batted it around until it fell onto the floor where the lid popped off and the grease spilled out. Down to the floor and into the grease went King Carlos, sniffing and licking and slipping and sliding. Larissa did not know about any of this because she and Aaron were busy working on their relationship. Neither did Larissa realize the storm had passed, because she knew of nothing at that moment but Aaron Wolf.

King Carlos seemed to tire of walking around in the grease, so he went into the living room and lay down upon the bear rug. In doing so, he tracked bacon grease from the kitchen, through the dining room, and onto Brother Bear. Then King Carlos began fervently licking his paws. When they were clean, he went back into the kitchen and walked around in the grease again. Apparently tiring of this, he returned to the bear rug. He did this off and on all night long.

Larissa would have been very unhappy with King Carlos if she had known what terrible messes he was making in her house. But Larissa did not know anything about her naughty cat because she and Aaron Wolf had spent most of the night sharing moments of mutual pleasure. The all-night activities must have been extremely exhausting for Larissa, Aaron, and King Carlos because all three slept most of the next day.

Chapter Ten

Larissa had just added some *piñon* logs to the fire when Aaron arrived at her house. He came over to the fireplace and warmed his hands. He stood next to her for a few moments and then reached over and kissed her cheek.

"Oh, your lips feel cold, Aaron." Larissa frowned.

"It's really getting cold outside. You need to warm me up." He put his arms around her and kissed her again.

Larissa pulled away from Aaron. "I want you to come out to the apartment with me. I have something I want to show you." She picked up her red shawl from the sofa and wrapped it around her shoulders.

Aaron followed her through the kitchen and out the back doorway. The air felt crisp and the night sky hinted at a spring snow. Larissa put her shawl up over her head as they walked across the courtyard. She quickly unlocked the apartment door. The apartment felt warm from the electric wall heater that Larissa had turned on earlier.

After flipping on a light switch, Larissa pointed to two large burlap bags lying on a table. "I want to know what to do with these. What I mean is, tell me the appropriate way to put them to rest."

Larissa picked up one of the bags, untied it, and held it open for Aaron to look inside. The bag had the word "female" crudely written on it with black ink.

Aaron looked into the bag. Without saying anything, he opened the second bag and peered into it.

"How did you get these?" He had a slight frown on his face.

"They've always been here. Well, not always here in the apartment. Most of the time they were in my father's den." Larissa looked down. "It has bothered me having them here for so many years in burlap bags. They are Native Americans. They need to be buried properly. They need to rest in peace."

"Yes, of course they do. But what do you know about them? And where did they come from?"

"I wish I knew where they are from, but I don't. For many years my father did a lot of digging at sites he discovered. I know he found things on his grandfather's land northeast of here."

"Why would he want these skeletal remains? What purpose did they serve him?" Aaron's voice seemed to have a somewhat angry tone to it.

"My father was inquisitive and very interested in the original people of this area just as you and I are."

Aaron reached into one of the bags and took out a skull and looked carefully at it. "So this is what an Indian's skull looks like." He shook his head. "You know this constitutes grave robbing, Larissa."

A twinge of guilt swept over her. "Yes, but I hope for a good purpose, not for any bad reason."

Larissa was well aware her father had been wrong in what he had done.

Aaron placed the skull back into the bag. "How would you like it if I dug up George Washington?"

Larissa wrinkled her brow and looked at Aaron. "I really wouldn't mind for a legitimate cause, such as providing more knowledge about something important. But your question is ridiculous because you must admit we already know an awful lot about George Washington and his contemporaries. I doubt that there is any reason to exhume his remains."

"I think you still wouldn't like it." Aaron sounded angry now.

"Why George Washington? You could have come up with someone a little more relevant. None of my ancestors came through the original thirteen colonies, or have you forgotten?" She paused and took a deep breath. "Look, Aaron, George Washington is your first president just as he is mine. You're an American just like I am."

"I doubt that." He began securing one of the bags. "You people violate our sacred lands, you dig up our ancestors, and you show no respect for us."

Larissa stood looking down at her feet. She was defenseless. Aaron finished securing the first bag.

Larissa pointed at the bags. "They are almost intact."

"What are intact?" Aaron finished securing the other bag.

"The two skeletal remains. The female lacks only a few phalanges. The male is missing his entire left foot."

Aaron looked grimly at Larissa. "Well, you must have known these two quite well." Then he picked up the bags and started toward the door.

Larissa, following him, turned out the light and locked the apartment door. "What are you going to do with them?" She failed to notice the light snow falling on the flagstones.

Aaron opened the courtyard gate. "I know someone who will take care of this problem for you." He went to his pickup and put the bags on the floorboard of the cab.

Larissa had followed him, but she suddenly turned away and ran back into the courtyard. She hurried into the house and flung herself face down on the sofa. It seemed impossible for her to stop her tears, and she let them flow freely as she sobbed into the sofa pillow. She did not know Aaron had entered the room until he sat down on the sofa and pulled her into his arms.

"What is it? Are you upset with me?" He spoke gently.

"No, it's not you. Something is making me sad, and I don't know what it is." She put her arms around him and held him tightly. "Aaron, please don't leave me tonight. I feel something is not right with me."

"Are you ill?"

"No. I just feel terribly sad. I can't explain it. Please, Aaron, don't leave me."

"I won't leave you." He laid her back down on the sofa. "I'll get blankets and pillows and make us a bed on the bear rug."

Larissa began shivering. "It's getting cold in here. Please add some wood to the fire and close the doors to the den and the bedrooms so it will get warmer in here."

King Carlos, who had been asleep in the middle of Larissa's bed, came into the living room and began meowing loudly. He turned around and walked to the kitchen continuing his noise. Larissa realized she had not fed her cat, so she immediately went into the kitchen and poured King Carlos a large helping of his favorite food. Then she opened a can of tuna fish, gave him a large spoonful and drained the oil from the can onto his dried food.

While Aaron made a bed in front of the fireplace, Larissa put on her warmest flannel pajamas.

Aaron smiled at Larissa when she returned to the living room. "I'll take off your favorite belt buckle." He pulled his belt out of the loops of his jeans.

Larissa lay down under the blankets on top of Brother Bear. She reached her hand out and softly rubbed the bear's head between its perpetually-opened eyes. As a child, Larissa took her naps here, usually with her hand on top of the bear's head. She often patted the bear, and even talked to the bear. Now as an adult, she still sensed a connection with the spirit of the bear.

"Turn out the lights and come lie down, Aaron. It's late and I'm so tired and sleepy." Larissa shivered again.

Aaron got under the blankets next to her. He took her in his arms and held her.

She caressed his cheek. "I've never felt such sadness before in my life, and I don't want to be alone, but I feel safe and secure when I'm with you."

Aaron pulled her closer and whispered, "Just go to sleep. I'll be right here, and I'll watch the fire and keep it going all night so we'll stay warm." He did not say anything for a while. Finally, he whispered, "I'm sorry if I upset you about George Washington. It wasn't a good example." He kissed Larissa on her forehead, then on her left cheek, and then on her right cheek. And in her ear he whispered, "Larissa, I love you."

Larissa did not hear this because she had fallen asleep. And while she slept, she had a dream about her childhood. In the dream, she knelt on a beautiful summer day on a bench at the picnic table in the courtyard. Her father stood behind her. On the table lay most of the bones from the burlap bag labeled "female."

"Here, Larissa, take this and put it where it belongs." Her father handed her one of the bones from the bag.

Larissa took the bone from her father's hand and looked carefully at it. "It's her tibia, Papá, and it goes here."

"Are you certain?" her father asked and smiled at her.

Larissa looked again at the bone. "Yes, Papá, I am certain." She laid the tibia in its proper position on the table.

"Good! You're correct and I am very proud of you." Her father kissed her on her forehead, then on her left cheek, and then on her right cheek. And in her ear he whispered, "Larissa, I love you."

Early the next morning Aaron arose and stirred the fire and added a few large chunks of pine wood. Larissa heard him and noticed he had dressed and had put on his jacket.

She sat up. "Are you leaving?"

"Yes, I need to get an early start so I can take care of your bags of bones."

"Aaron, listen to me. Those remains are more than just a bunch of bones to me. Those bones are all that's left of two people who once lived. They had feelings, needs, and desires just as you and I have." Larissa pushed back the covers and stood up. "The woman was about forty years old when she died. There are indications she had given birth, probably to several children. Toward the end of her life she must have been very malnourished. It shows in her bones."

Aaron did not speak but took a few steps toward Larissa.

She continued, "The man died at a younger age. He had a skull injury, but it didn't kill him because it had healed. He most likely died from a chest wound. You can see the damage in his ribs. Perhaps he died in battle. Maybe the man and woman knew one another, but I have no way of knowing." Larissa wiped a tear from her cheek.

"Yes, Aaron, I do know them well. I've known them all my life. They've taught me much, and I shall miss them."

Aaron took her in his arms. "I'll take care of everything." He kissed her on her forehead, then on her left cheek, and then on her right cheek. And in her ear he whispered, "I meant what I said last night."

Larissa did not understand the meaning of these words, and she did not ask Aaron to explain. She walked with him to the door and watched him leave. Then she lay back down on top of Brother Bear, covered herself with the wool blankets, and grieved for the man and woman whose remains Aaron had taken away forever.

Chapter Eleven

It was Saturday night at La Llorona Cantina, and a *conjunto* made up of the three Jaramillo brothers played loudly in the adjoining dance hall. Larissa had been sitting on a bar stool since eight-thirty chatting with Braulio and Mimi as they worked behind the bar. From time to time Larissa glanced up at the big clock hanging on the wall beside the Bull Durham Tobacco sign.

"It's already ten o'clock," she said to Mimi, "and Aaron's more than an hour late. He must not be coming."

Mimi looked up, raised her eyebrows, and continued her work.

As Larissa finished drinking her fourth glass of ginger ale, she tapped her foot to the beat of a polka. She loved to dance the old dances her father had taught her, especially *La Varsoviana, El Chotis*, and the polka. On nights like this one, she missed her father terribly.

Larissa pushed her empty glass toward Braulio. "If Aaron comes in, please tell him I'm in the dance hall."

As soon as Larissa walked into the hall, Victor Galván, one of the Saturday night regulars, asked her to dance. The polka soon ended, so Victor and Larissa stayed on the dance floor for the next dance, a waltz. Larissa always enjoyed dancing with the older man. When the waltz finished, Victor gave Larissa a hug and a kiss on the forehead and told her thank you. He almost always did this, and she thought nothing of it. As Larissa left the dance floor, she noticed Aaron standing against the wall holding a bottle of beer and staring at her.

Smiling, she went over to him. "I'm glad you made it. I had decided you weren't coming."

"Yes, I see you had. Who's the man you were kissing?" Aaron did not look very pleased.

"I didn't kiss anyone. You saw Victor Galván give me a kiss on the forehead for dancing with him."

Aaron took a big swallow of beer. "And what else does he give you?"

"I don't know what you mean. Are you jealous of one of my father's friends?" Aaron's words had surprised her. "Because if you are jealous of an old friend, then I'm sorry for you because you have little confidence in yourself and even less in me." She turned away from him and faced the dance floor to watch the couples dance.

As they continued standing without talking, Aaron finished his beer. He then tightly took hold of Larissa by her arm. "Come over here to the bar. I've had a little trouble with the bartender. You know—your big friend Braulio?"

"What kind of trouble?"

Aaron did not reply. Larissa went into the cantina with him, and they walked up to the bar.

"I'd like another beer," Aaron said to Braulio and laid money on the bar.

Braulio got Aaron a beer and set it in front of him, but did not take any of Aaron's money.

"How much do I owe you?" Aaron asked and picked up his money and held it out to Braulio.

"Nothing," Braulio said and turned away.

Larissa quickly said, "Aaron, my guests don't pay. Is this the problem you had with Braulio?" She was finding this frustrating. "You know Mimi and I own this business. I didn't invite you here to have you pay for anything." Larissa forced a smile, hoping to smooth the situation.

Aaron did not respond, and his face remained expressionless as he drank his beer. Larissa sat on the bar stool next to where Aaron stood, observing him as he drank the beer. They did not talk and Aaron seemed to be avoiding eye contact with her.

Finally, Larissa slid down from the stool and touched him on his shoulder. "Aaron, let's play pool." She pointed to the pool table just a few feet away from where they were standing.

"No, I don't play pool with women." He did not look at her.

"Then let's go dance. You do dance with women, don't you?"

Aaron seemed to ignore her and ordered another beer. Braulio served him, and Aaron turned and looked at Larissa. "I'm sorry. You already know I'm not a good dancer. I never learned how. Go dance with your friend." Aaron's speech seemed a little labored.

"Aaron, I hate to say this, but I think you've had enough to drink." She laid her hand on his arm.

He pulled away from her, took a long drink from the beer bottle, and then said, "Yes, Miss Anthropologist, I know what you're going to say. We Indians can't hold our liquor. It's our bad metabolism. You think we're all alike, don't you?"

"No, I don't think any such thing. Besides, I don't believe those metabolism myths." She put her hand on Aaron's arm. "I think you don't need to drink any more beer, so I'm going to drive you to my house and make us some coffee."

Aaron turned away, and Larissa went to the end of the bar and told Braulio she would be driving Aaron to her house in Aaron's pickup. She gave Braulio the keys to her van and asked him to bring it home after he closed the cantina. When she turned around, she saw Aaron going out the front entrance with Trixie Trujillo leading him by the hand. This did not please Larissa at all.

She hurried out of the building in time to see Aaron and Trixie disappear around the corner. Larissa followed them and noticed Aaron's pickup parked about half-way down the block. By the time she got to the pickup, Trixie had already pushed Aaron up against the side of the vehicle. Trixie put her arms around Aaron's waist and pulled his wallet out of a back pocket of his jeans.

Larissa grabbed the wallet from Trixie's hand. "Get away from him before I call the police."

Trixie did not move, so Larissa took her by the upper arm and pulled her away from Aaron. Giving Larissa a sneer, Trixie turned and began walking quickly back toward the corner.

"Aaron, hold still!" Larissa tried to put his wallet into one of his back pockets.

Aaron grasped Larissa by the shoulders and pushed her out in front of him. "Well, Larissa Lozoya, I think you're jealous of that woman. I'm sorry you don't have any confidence in yourself.

You're just like me—no self-confidence." Then he pulled her to him and tried to kiss her, but she avoided it by turning her face away from him.

Attempting to put Aaron's wallet back into his pocket, and trying to keep him from kissing her, caused Larissa not to see the man wearing a black suit and a broad-brimmed hat getting out of a car across the street. She also failed to see him walk up behind her.

"Please put the wallet on the pickup hood," the man said as he held up a badge apparently for Larissa's benefit.

Larissa quickly turned to see a tall man scowling at her. Larissa laid Aaron's wallet on the hood of the pickup.

"Show me some identification," the man said to Larissa.

Larissa put her hand to her pocket. "Sorry, I must have left it in the cantina. Want me to go get it?" Larissa started to walk away

"No, you stay right here and tell me your name," the man replied.

Larissa hesitated, and then loudly said, "I don't recognize you, so you tell me your name first. And just what kind of a cop are you anyway?"

"You don't need to know my name. All you need to know is that I'm a bounty hunter, I have a warrant for your arrest, and I'm here to take you back to Colorado, Miss Trujillo. Right? You are Maria Teresa Trujillo, aren't you?"

"No, I'm not Maria Teresa anybody. You're talking about Trixie!" Larissa said loudly.

At that, Aaron spoke up, "Hey, her name isn't Maria Teresa."

The bounty hunter quickly turned toward Aaron. "And you—show me your identification."

Aaron took his wallet off the hood of the pickup and began fumbling with its contents.

The man turned back to Larissa. "And you, Miss Trujillo. Do you usually work this street?"

Larissa bristled. "I'm not Trixie Trujillo and I'm not a prostitute if that's what you're implying."

Aaron handed the bounty hunter his driver's license.

"How much money do you have in there?" The bounty hunter pointed to Aaron's wallet.

Aaron fumbled through his wallet again. "I don't have very much. I guess about twelve dollars."

The bounty hunter looked at Aaron's driver's license and then handed it back to Aaron. "Wolf—not a local name, is it?"

"No, it isn't. I'm from Oklahoma." Aaron's speech sounded a little slurred.

"Well, maybe you'd better go back to Oklahoma. This town isn't friendly toward drunk Indians. You almost lost your money to this little chippie." The bounty hunter gave Larissa a nasty look.

Larissa took a step toward the man. "How dare you call me a chippie," she said and gave him a nastier look.

"I'm surprised the local cops haven't arrested your lady friend here, Mr. Wolf. Did she offer you any kind of sexual favors for money?"

"I don't sell sexual favors!" Larissa yelled at the man.

Aaron had a puzzled look on his face. "She never asks me to pay her for anything. And what she and I do is none of your business, anyway."

Larissa moved closer to the bounty hunter and shook her finger in his face. "You're making a big mistake."

At that point, the bounty hunter took a pair of handcuffs from his belt. "Turn around Miss Trujillo and put your hands behind your back."

Larissa could not hold back her defiance. "I will not do that! I'm not a prostitute! I don't know you! You're not from around here, and who do you think you are anyway?" She looked the man squarely in the face.

"My name is Rubén Silva, and I'm taking you back to Colorado, and if you don't like it, then you shouldn't have jumped bail."

"You're crazy! Why don't you arrest Trixie Trujillo? She's the one who took Aaron's wallet out of his pocket! She's the prostitute, not me!"

Rubén Silva grasped Larissa by the hands, and forcing her arms behind her, he put the handcuffs on her wrists. Aaron stood leaning against his pickup looking somewhat bewildered by what Silva had just done to Larissa. Silva began pushing Larissa across the street to his car.

"Aaron! Aaron! Do something!" Larissa yelled.

However, Aaron did nothing but stand motionless watching Rubén Silva put Larissa in the back seat of his car and drive away with her. Larissa never looked at Aaron. If she had, she would have seen him hurrying toward the front of the cantina. However, Larissa saw nothing but the back of Rubén Silva's head as she let him know how incompetent and foolish he would appear when she sued him for falsely arresting her.

Rubén Silva did not say anything while he drove Larissa to the Los Espíritus Police Station. On the other hand, Larissa emitted a continuous barrage of loud protest. She did not shut up until she was inside the police station where seeing Frankie Nelson sitting at the desk relieved some of her anxiety. Frankie, who had joined the police force on the day after he graduated from high school, had first professed his love for Larissa when they were in the third grade. Over the years, Frankie had hounded Larissa to date him, but she always refused. Even when away at school, Larissa received many letters from the lovesick Frankie. Finally he gave up, married a girl from Española, and became the father of six children. Now, Larissa stood before him with her hands secured behind her back.

"I found her outside La Llorona Cantina rolling a drunk Indian," Rubén Silva said as he set a warrant on Frankie's desk. "I think she's probably soliciting there at the cantina. This town needs to do something about these prostitutes you've got here." Rubén Silva walked over to the coffee pot and poured himself a cup of very black coffee.

Frankie Nelson looked at Larissa and began laughing.

Silva stopped stirring his coffee and looked at Frankie Nelson. "Can you keep her here until tomorrow when I can transport her back to Colorado?"

"I'm sorry, Mr. Silva. This woman is Larissa Lasoya. She owns La Llorona Cantina. And tell me this, did the Indian have braids and go by the name of Wolf?" Frankie asked. "Because if he did, he's her boyfriend, and Larissa Lozoya is not a prostitute, she's a college professor."

Rubén Silva did not say a word, but glared at Larissa who stood looking at him with a big smirk on her face. Then quickly, he reached in his shirt pocket and pulled out a piece of note paper, "Did you say Lozoya? How do you spell that?" He continued looking at the paper as Frankie spelled the name.

Suddenly Larissa remembered Aaron and said, "Frankie, listen to me. Trixie took Aaron Wolf's wallet, but I got it away from her. Aaron's had too much to drink. We left him on the street by the cantina, so please call Braulio and tell him to go outside and find Aaron."

"I'll take care of it." Frankie picked up the telephone receiver.

Rubén Silva unlocked the handcuffs and removed them. Larissa gave Silva a dirty look.

He then narrowed his eyes and sneered at her. "I still think you might be guilty of something, Miss Lozoya," he said in a low voice and picked up the warrant from Frankie's desk.

"And I still think you're incompetent," Larissa said loudly.

Silva picked up his cup of coffee, and walked out the front entrance of the police station just as Mimi walked in.

"Is Aaron okay?" Larissa asked immediately.

"Yes, Victor Galván drove Aaron home and Victor's brother followed them in Aaron's pickup." Mimi turned to Frankie. "Why can't the police department do something about those prostitutes? Just look at what Trixie caused tonight by taking Aaron outside and stealing his wallet."

Larissa quickly asked Mimi, "How did you find out about Trixie taking Aaron's wallet?"

"Aaron told me when he came back in to get help for you. He may have been drinking, but he knew exactly what had happened." Mimi turned to Frankie and said, "I'm taking her home now." Then Mimi grasped Larissa by the arm and began walking her toward the door. "Aaron seemed very upset about what happened to you, but I told him I'd come to the police station and take care of the problem."

Larissa snorted loudly. "He can't possibly be as upset as I am. I don't even want to hear his stupid excuse for going outside with that ugly, pimply-faced Trixie. I don't want to hear anything from him." Larissa stomped out of the police station.

Mimi took Larissa back to the cantina, and Larissa got her keys from Braulio and drove home. As she walked into her house, the telephone was ringing. She answered and heard Aaron's voice.

"Larissa, I'm so sorry. Are you okay?" Aaron sounded his usual self.

"I'm fine, and I need to go to bed."

"I want to come over."

"No, I'm not interested in drunkards. I'm going to hang up, Aaron."

"No, Larissa, listen to me, please. I don't know what happened to me tonight. I had already had some beers with Eloy before I came to the cantina."

"Then you were foolish to drink more beer," Larissa said.

"I know I shouldn't have drunk more. I don't even like the taste of it very much. And I sure didn't like seeing another man dancing with you and kissing you."

"Grow up, Aaron."

"And another thing, I don't like you paying for my beer. I can buy my own. What kind of a man do you think I am?"

"I think right now you're a silly man. And you need to go to bed. Don't call me again tonight. In fact, I don't even know if I ever want to talk to you again." Larissa slammed the telephone receiver down.

She was too exhausted to take a shower, so she just undressed and got into bed. King Carlos lay asleep on the pillow next to hers. Sleep would not come for Larissa because she kept turning the events of the evening over and over in her mind. She had never before seen Aaron drink too much, and he seemed so terribly helpless. This frightened her. And Rubén Silva had acted very arrogant with

127

her. He did not even apologize. And he had said he thought her to be guilty of something anyway. All of this angered her. Maybe she would call an attorney on Monday and see if she had enough grounds for a lawsuit against Silva.

No matter how hard she tried, Larissa could not go to sleep. The music of the Jaramillo brothers kept playing in her head, and she could not rid her mind of the thought of Aaron walking out of the cantina with Trixie Trujillo. What Aaron had said about paying for his own beer concerned her. Perhaps because she had made him feel inadequate, he had walked out with Trixie. This puzzled Larissa. However, she knew for sure she wanted Aaron to love her and to tell her he loved her. Now she thought it might not ever happen. Carmelita's prophecy must have been wrong.

Larissa began crying, and her loud sobbing seemed to have disturbed the sleeping King Carlos because he meowed loudly and jumped off the bed and walked into the hallway. He stopped and looked back at her.

Larissa suddenly remembered something. "I'm sorry. I forgot to feed you tonight."

She got up and put on her robe and went to the kitchen and poured cat food into King Carlos's bowl. As King Carlos ate, Larissa sat at the kitchen table and watched him.

"My dear King Carlos, things aren't going well. I'm not sure about anything anymore and especially about Aaron Wolf."

Chapter Twelve

The day after Larissa's encounter with Rubén Silva, she stayed in bed. She did not sleep much because she continued to ponder the things that had happened the night before. She hoped Aaron would call her but it did not happen. She had told him not to and now she was regretting it.

On Monday she was sure he would make an effort to see her, but he did not. By Tuesday night she suspected she had been too harsh with him. By the time she got home from work on Wednesday afternoon without seeing or hearing from Aaron, she was in a depressed mood. She feared she would lose him if she did not do something quickly to let him know she still cared.

Late Wednesday evening someone knocked loudly on the front door, startling Larissa as she sat alone eating a tuna fish sandwich for supper. Thinking it was Aaron, she hurried and eagerly opened the door. However, she looked into the smiling face of Rubén Silva. In one of his hands, he held a large bouquet of red roses.

"Good evening, Miss Lozoya. How are you?" He tipped his black hat with his free hand. "These are for you." He handed Larissa the bouquet.

She took the roses, looked at them, then looked at Rubén Silva. "What are these for?"

"They are to help me apologize for treating you so unfairly on Saturday night." He smiled. "May I come in for a moment? I need to talk with you."

Larissa stepped aside and allowed the man to come in.

He removed his hat. "I'm sorry I mistook you for something other than the beautiful, upstanding member of this community that you are."

Larissa did not respond to this remark, but said, "Let me put these roses in water. Come on in." She led him into the kitchen.

She gestured for him to sit at the table as she laid the roses on the counter. Finding a large vase under the sink, she filled it with water. She noted the brown-haired bounty hunter appeared handsome and reminded her a little of Aaron, although Aaron had darker skin and hair.

"Would you like a tuna fish sandwich, Mr. Silva?" Larissa asked as she arranged the roses in the vase.

"Thank you, no, but I would like to take you to dinner tonight if you'll allow me." He sat back in the chair and smiled.

"No, thank you. I've already eaten, and I think the roses and dinner are just part of your scheme to keep me from suing you." Larissa frowned and riveted her eyes on his. "I don't take you seriously at all, Mr. Silva. And I really might sue you."

His lips hinted at a smile. "I'm sorry you feel this way because even if we had not have had the bad experience on Saturday night, I would still want to take you out. And please call me Rubén."

"Well, Rubén, I'm not free to go out with you. I have a boyfriend. You told him to go back to

Oklahoma. Remember?" Larissa put the vase of roses on the kitchen table.

Rubén looked at Larissa with raised eyebrows. "How well do you know Aaron Wolf?"

"I've known him since this past summer. We spend quite a bit of time together. Why do you ask?" Larissa wiped some water from the table with a dish towel.

"You do know he's married, don't you?" Rubén's face did not change.

These words stunned Larissa.

She hesitated a moment, and then slowly said, "No, I'm sure he's not married." She hesitated again, and then forced herself to sound more confident as she continued, "He and his fiancée broke up several years ago. A colleague of mine who knew Aaron at that time told me this."

Rubén Silva looked at Larissa and frowned. "He doesn't live alone. You know that don't you?"

"What do you mean? Of course, he lives alone." Larissa was beginning to feel a little shaky.

Rubén smiled. "He lives with his wife and two children here in Los Espíritus. And he's been married twice. He has an ex-wife and two children in Oklahoma."

Larissa pulled out a chair and sat down. She said haltingly, "This is hard to believe."

Larissa looked at Rubén Silva, and then she looked down and closed her eyes. Her heart was beating rapidly and her breathing was labored. She was remembering the time she took clean clothes to Aaron at the hospital and the nurse told Larissa a woman had already brought him some clothing.

Later, when Larissa had asked Aaron for his home telephone number, he said he had no telephone. He explained that he usually called her from a nearby public phone. All of this raced through Larissa's mind. Perhaps he lied because he did not want Larissa calling his home, especially if he had a wife. Maybe Rubén Silva was telling the truth, and if so, she had been cruelly violated by Aaron. Larissa realized that if what Rubén Silva had said was true, then she was a fool. She began to softly cry.

Rubén quickly arose and, putting his hands on Larissa's upper arms, pulled her up and put his arms around her. "I'm so sorry. I did not know it would hit you so hard." He held her against his chest and gently patted her on her back.

Larissa stood for a while in Rubén's arms and wept. Suddenly she sensed the fragrance of bay rum. She stopped crying and closed her eyes and just stood, taking in the scent which reminded her of the man she loved.

Finally, Larissa stepped back from Rubén Silva. "I'll have to have some proof, before I'll believe Aaron is married. I'm sure you're mistaken."

"I've requested proof. It should be here tomorrow or the next day. And tell me, have you ever been to Wolf's house?"

"No, I've never needed to go to Aaron's house, but he told me where he lived."

"Well, maybe you might just quietly drive by his house and see if a woman and children seem to be living there. Maybe you'll see children's toys in the yard." From his jacket pocket, Rubén took a card and a pen and wrote Aaron's address.

Larissa took the card and looked at it through her tears. "Thank you," she whispered. "Maybe I should just ask him if he's married."

"No, don't do that. You may anger him, and I don't want you to get hurt. Just give me a few days to get the evidence you need," Rubén said and smiled at Larissa. "In the meanwhile, I think you should stay away from him."

He started to leave, but turned around. "By the way, Larissa, Assistant Chief Nelson said you might have an apartment for rent. I'm having to stay here in Los Espíritus for a short time and would like to rent your apartment if I can."

"Well, I don't know." Larissa hesitated to say yes.

"It's only for a month or so. Nelson said he'd vouch for me. Just call him." Rubén smiled. "And I'll pay you whatever you want."

Larissa took Rubén out to the apartment and showed it to him. He said he liked it and would move in the next day if she would agree to it. She said he could rent the apartment, and they could work out the details the next day. She really wanted Rubén Silva to leave so she could drive by the address he had given her.

After Rubén Silva left, Larissa got into her van and drove to a house in a low-rent neighborhood. Larissa did not see Aaron's pickup anywhere. She turned down a side street and parked her van where she could keep her eyes on the small stucco house. She noticed a child's wagon and a tricycle in the yard.

After waiting for about half an hour, Larissa saw Aaron's pickup pull into the driveway. Aaron got out and took a large grocery bag from the back end of the pickup. A nearby street light lit up the driveway, and Larissa had no trouble recognizing Aaron. Then Larissa saw a woman and two small children get out from the passenger side. The woman also took out a large grocery bag from the back of the pickup. Then all four persons went into the house. Larissa drove home, fed King Carlos, and went to bed.

* * *

The next day, Larissa looked often out her office window at Aaron's pickup parked in the faculty lot. She wanted to find out if Aaron had a home telephone number on file with the history department. However, she did not want to take a chance of him knowing she would resort to spying. Finally, late in the afternoon, Larissa no longer saw Aaron's pickup parked in the lot.

Thinking the secretary would not give out Aaron's home phone number over the telephone, Larissa hurried to the history department. The secretary seemed to believe the story Larissa told her about needing Aaron's home telephone number. Larissa hoped the secretary would tell her that Aaron had no home telephone. Her hopes were dashed when the woman wrote down the number and handed the slip of paper to Larissa. Larissa took the slip of paper directly to her office and called the number.

When a woman answered, Larissa asked, "Is Dr. Wolf available?"

"No, I'm sorry. He's not in. May I tell him who called?" the woman replied in a friendly manner.

"Oh, no thank you. I'm just one of his students. It's not important." Larissa hung up the receiver.

She sat back in her desk chair and shut her eyes tightly. Her world was falling down around her. How could she have been so stupid? She had been a fool, and she continued to be a fool because she still loved Aaron Wolf. After putting the slip of paper with Aaron's telephone number into her pocket, she got up from her desk, locked the building, and walked home.

She found Rubén Silva sitting in his car waiting for her. He had another dozen roses and a few personal possessions which he needed to move into the apartment. Larissa took the roses and led Rubén to the kitchen.

"Please quit spending so much money on roses for me." She got out another vase and filled it with water.

"I'm not spending much of my money on roses. Besides, I've got plenty to spend on you. Remember, I don't have wives and children to support." He smiled at Larissa.

She gave him one of the keys to the apartment from the key holder on the kitchen wall and offered to help him move his things in.

He put his hand on her shoulder and said, "No, I have very few things. Get ready and I'll take you to dinner."

Larissa forced a smile, but did not say anything. She wanted to go to bed and sleep, but she also wanted to go to dinner with Rubén. In truth, she really did not want dinner, she just wanted to stand near him, close her eyes, and smell the scent of his bay rum. Finally, she agreed to go to dinner.

Larissa put on her prettiest dress and a pair of high heels. She carefully applied her make-up and curled the ends of her hair. When she looked at her reflection in the full-length mirror on her bedroom door, she liked what she saw. *Just look at what Aaron Wolf is never going to have,* she thought. Then she remembered she would never have Aaron Wolf. Before she could think anymore about her situation, Rubén knocked on the kitchen door ready to take her to the nicest restaurant in Los Espíritus.

Rubén insisted on buying Larissa the most expensive entrée on the menu. He also ordered a costly bottle of wine. They ate slowly and talked, mostly about Larissa because Rubén asked her many personal questions. He answered all the questions Larissa asked him. He revealed he originally came from southern Colorado, was divorced with no children. He had earned a university degree in business and had been a bounty hunter for fifteen years.

After dinner, Rubén took Larissa home and told her he wanted to show her something he had received that day. He went out to the apartment and returned to Larissa's living room with some documents.

"This is a copy of Wolf's last year's IRS tax return." He held a form out to Larissa. "See, it's a joint return with his wife, Madeline Wolf. And look at the names of his dependents."

Larissa took the copy of the tax return and read the names. His dependents were Rosa Wolf, ex-wife, and four children. Larissa handed the form back to Rubén without saying anything.

"You need to quit thinking about him, Larissa. He's no good for you." Rubén folded the IRS form several times and put it into his jacket pocket. "You don't deserve to be treated this way."

Larissa dropped down onto the sofa. She put her hands over her face and began to sob. Rubén quickly sat down beside her and took her in his arms.

"Go ahead and cry, Larissa. Get him out of your system."

Rubén began kissing Larissa on her cheek. She smelled his skin, it smelled like Aaron's. She put her arms around Rubén and closed her eyes. She pretended he was Aaron.

She whispered in his ear, "Please, hold me. I just want you to hold me."

He put his lips on her cheek and moved them slowly to her lips. For a moment it was as if Aaron was holding her, and it was wonderful.

"Aaron," she whispered in Rubén's ear.

Rubén pushed Larissa away from him.

"What's the matter with you, woman? Am I not good enough for you?"

Larissa realized too late what she had done. "I'm sorry. I meant to say something to you about Aaron, but I decided not to." She hoped she had covered her mistake.

Rubén took her by the shoulders and began kissing her roughly on her mouth. She attempted to push him away from her. He became insistent and forcibly held her.

"Stop it," Larissa said loudly and finally pushed him up.

Rubén sat back on the sofa breathing heavily. "What's wrong with you? I bring you flowers. I take you to dinner. I expect a little more from you."

"And I expect you to be a gentleman." Larissa stood up and looked down at him.

Rubén gave her the same sneer he had given her the night he had arrested her. "Tell me something, woman. Would you rather have the drunk Indian instead of me?"

"Yes, I would," Larissa quickly replied and then wondered if she should have spoken the truth to this man who seemed very angry with her.

"Well, I see for sure now you're not a prostitute. You're just a whore, and I hate whores worse than I hate prostitutes." Rubén stood up.

Larissa stepped aside so Rubén could leave. "Good night, Rubén. Maybe tomorrow you'll be in a better mood."

Larissa followed him to the back door and locked it when he left. Then she went into her bedroom and got undressed. She saw the slip of paper with Aaron's telephone number on it lying on the dresser. As she put it into the drawer of the bedside table, the telephone rang.

She answered it and heard Aaron say, "Larissa, I'm sorry about everything that happened. Can you forgive me for drinking too much?"

Larissa did not hesitate to answer. "Yes, I can forgive you for getting drunk. That doesn't even bother me very much. What does bother me is the fact you have too many women and children." Larissa spoke in an angry manner.

"I told you when we first met that I had obligations," Aaron said.

"You didn't tell me you had a damned harem!" Larissa raised her voice. "And just where are you calling me from since you claim not to have a home telephone?"

"I just got the phone installed last week. I didn't have enough money until recently for the big deposit the telephone company required." Aaron sounded a little distressed. "Let me give you the number now."

"I don't want your telephone number. Aren't you afraid I might call your house and your wife will answer?" Larissa's stomach began to churn, and a burning sensation crept up her esophagus.

Aaron hesitated. "Wife? Larissa, what are you talking about?"

Larissa suddenly became dizzy, and she sat down on the side of the bed to keep from falling. "You made a fool of me, but you won't do it again." A wave of nausea swept over her. She hung up the telephone receiver and ran into her bathroom where she vomited up the most expensive meal she had eaten in a long, long time.

Chapter Thirteen

Larissa had not seen Rubén Silva since the previous night. Neither had she seen King Carlos all evening, so she began making a systematic search of the house, checking the cat's favorite hiding places. After about an hour, it was obvious to Larissa that he must have gone out when she had opened the back door earlier in the day. As long as the gate stayed closed, he could not get out of the courtyard, and, without front claws, he would have difficulty climbing adobe walls as well as tall wooden gates.

Thinking he must be in the courtyard, Larissa opened the back door and called to him. He did not come, but he usually did not respond when she called him unless he wanted something to eat. Night was approaching, and Larissa wanted King Carlos in the house. There was also a sense of urgency eating at her because Mimi had asked her to come tonight to the cantina, and Larissa suspected that it had something to do with Aaron.

Earlier in the day, Larissa had told Mimi everything that had happened with Rubén Silva. Mimi insisted something was really suspicious about the story regarding Aaron's two wives and four children. Mimi said she did not trust anything that Rubén Silva said, and she doubted Rubén could have acquired Aaron's tax papers so quickly. According to Mimi, Aaron needed a chance to defend himself, or at least to explain everything.

Larissa looked forward to confronting Aaron and venting some of the angry feelings that she harbored. But first she needed to find King Carlos so she could leave knowing he was safe in the house.

Larissa walked out into the courtyard and looked around. Suddenly, she saw King Carlos sitting inside the apartment on the window sill. He was looking out at her.

"You naughty boy, how did you get in there?" Larissa tried the doorknob, but the door was locked, and she knew Rubén wasn't there. She rushed into her house and came back with a key, and let herself into the apartment.

King Carlos jumped down from the window and came over to Larissa and began weaving in and out of her ankles. She stepped over some papers strewn on the floor just inside the doorway. Probably something King Carlos has done, she assumed, as she turned on the overhead light and bent down and retrieved the papers.

When she laid the papers on a nearby table she noticed two file folders, one bearing her name and the other Aaron's name. She opened Aaron's and saw several pages of handwritten notes which she quickly perused. The names of Madeline and Rosa appeared and were listed as Aaron's sisters. Four other names were listed with either nephew or niece noted after each name. This troubled Larissa because the tax return form that Rubén had shown her the night before listed Madeline and Rosa as Aaron's wives.

Larissa quickly looked inside the other folder. It contained a collection of documents pertaining to her and her father. There were copies of her father's will, deeds to her father's properties and the house, and a document naming Larissa as part owner of La Llorona Cantina and Dance Hall. She also saw copies of bank statements and several IRS return forms, some hers and some her father's. Her heart began beating rapidly and her breath came quick and jerky. Something appeared wrong, something seemed strange and sinister. Mimi must have been right about Rubén Silva.

Larissa arranged the papers and the folders and left them on the table. She took King Carlos into her arms and walked out of the apartment just as Rubén Silva stepped into the courtyard.

"What were you doing in the apartment?" Rubén snapped at her.

"I was just letting my cat out. I'm sorry. I don't know how he got in there." She was a little unsure of the situation as she began moving toward the back door of her house.

"He's a nosy cat," Rubén said and frowned at Larissa. "Maybe you're nosy, too."

Larissa moved faster. "Good night, Rubén. I'm tired. I'm going to bed early."

"You better not have been too nosy, Larissa. If you were, you'll be sorry." He went into the apartment just as Larissa entered her house.

She closed the back door, locked it and carefully drew the curtain across the door's glass window. Still holding the cat in her arms, she went into the living room to lock the front door. King Carlos seemed to be acting strangely and appeared nervous. She put him down and walked back to the kitchen with King Carlos following her. She put food into his bowl and spoke softly to him as she stroked his back. Suddenly, there came a loud knock on the back door. Larissa jumped and King Carlos arched his back and spat. Then neither she nor the cat moved. The knock came again followed by Rubén's loud voice.

"Larissa, open the door! I know you're in there!"

Larissa walked quietly across the kitchen to the dining room doorway. Behind her she heard the outside door to the den open. King Carlos must have heard it also, because he walked toward the den and sat down in the doorway and looked into the darkened room. Larissa was certain she had not unlocked the outside door to the den in weeks. Then a noise came from the den. Maybe Rubén had taken the key from where she kept it hanging on the key holder.

She did not have time to check the key holder because she turned and saw Rubén Silva standing in the den looking at her. Larissa picked up King Carlos, rushed to her bedroom, and closed the door and locked it. Then she opened the drawer of the bedside table and took out the slip of paper on which Aaron's home telephone number was written. She picked up the telephone receiver and dialed the number. A woman answered and Larissa asked for Aaron.

"He's not home. Can I tell him who called?"

Rubén began pounding on Larissa's bedroom door.

"It's Larissa Lozoya. Please. I need Aaron. Find him. Hurry! Rubén Silva is breaking into my bedroom!"

Rubén was now kicking the door. The door popped open, and a seemingly enraged Rubén rushed into the bedroom. As he slammed the door shut, Larissa dropped the telephone receiver between the bed and the bedside table. She realized too late she had made a mistake by calling Aaron's house instead of the police department.

"Why don't you want to talk to me?" Rubén asked with a sneer on his face. "Is it because you were nosy?"

"Get out of my bedroom!" Larissa yelled.

Rubén quickly moved toward her and grabbed a handful of her hair and forced her down onto the bed. She tried to escape his hold, but she proved no match for him. He easily held her down and ripped the front of her blouse open.

"Where's your drunk Indian boyfriend? Why isn't he here to protect you?" Rubén slapped Larissa across the face.

She felt blood oozing from her left nostril. Her head seemed to be spinning. Then she heard herself whimpering while Rubén, quickly handcuffed her wrists behind her back.

Larissa tried to regain her composure. "Rubén Silva, stop this nonsense," she said almost calmly. "Take these cuffs off me. You don't have to do this to have sex with me."

"I don't want to have sex with you, you dirty little whore. I want to know what you did with the money." He released his grip on her.

Larissa raised her body up from the bed and looked at him. "What money? What are you talking about?"

"You know damn well what money. The money your father found when he was digging up Indian burial sites." Rubén hit her in the face with his fist causing her to fall backwards across the bed.

For a few moments Larissa lost consciousness. When her senses returned, she felt blood running from both of her nostrils. She quickly became aware that Rubén had removed a large hunting knife from the scabbard that he wore on his belt. He now held it just above her face. As she tried to move out from beneath him, she felt the handcuffs painfully cutting into her wrists.

"For God sake, Rubén Silva, loosen these handcuffs!" Larissa said loudly as he held her down with one hand and laid the blade of the knife flat against her skin just above the waistband of her jeans.

"Tell me where the money is, Larissa, and I won't hurt you," he whispered.

"You are hurting me now!" Larissa screamed.

Rubén dragged the flat side of the blade slowly up Larissa's torso, stopping just below her left breast. Larissa held her breath, and she did not move. She looked at his face and saw him glaring at her. He then lifted the blade and moved it to her left shoulder where he slipped it under the bra strap and cut it. She flinched and the blade painfully cut her skin.

"If you move, I may cut you again," Rubén whispered. He rubbed his finger across the cut, smearing her blood. "Just tell me where the money is and I'll let you up." He put the knife blade under the strap on the other side, hesitated, and loudly laughed. He cut the strap.

"Rubén, why are you doing this to me?" Larissa's voice was trembling.

"You know what I want from you. The money your father stole. That's all—nothing more" He placed the point of the knife on the exposed skin of her left breast. "Give me the money or I'll carve my initials in you."

Larissa felt the point of the knife as it pricked her skin. Looking at Rubén as he hovered just above her, Larissa saw a crazed look on his face. Then she heard a woman screaming, and, for a few moments, she failed to realize she was listening to herself.

Rubén slapped Larissa across the face. "Shut your mouth, or I'll really hurt you." He took the knife and hacked off a handful of her hair. "I think I'll give you a nice haircut. Let's see how your boyfriend likes you then."

Larissa began kicking and attempting to get away from her assailant. As she fought against him, he hacked at her hair, and the knife nicked and sliced her scalp and face in a number of places. She became desperate and began a frantic attempt to get away from the man whom she now realized was capable of just about anything.

At sometime while Larissa was screaming and kicking, King Carlos jumped up onto the bed.

Although Larissa's eyes had become nearly swollen shut, she saw Rubén grab King Carlos and hurl him across the room. Larissa quit screaming just in time to hear the air go out of King Carlos's lungs as the cat hit the wall on the other side of the room. Then she heard King Carlos hit the floor with a loud thud. The cat jumped to his feet and quickly ran under the bed.

Rubén bent over Larissa and laid the knife blade on her abdomen. "Now, where was I? Oh, yes, I was going to carve my initials into your beautiful skin."

Just then King Carlos came out from under the bed and ran toward the closed door. The cat turned and hissed, and then sat down and looked at Rubén. Rubén turned away from Larissa and slowly walked over to the dressing table where he picked up the silver hairbrush that had belonged to María Lourdes Gálvez de Lozoya. He looked at it, laid it down and picked up the silver hand mirror.

Rubén chuckled and said, "Look, *gato*. I've got something for you."

Rubén threw the mirror, but King Carlos avoided being hit by quickly running back under the bed. Larissa heard the mirror shatter into many pieces as it hit the floor. However, she did not hear the breaking of glass in the kitchen door because she heard only herself screaming as she frantically tried to get off the bed. She did not see the large man come into her bedroom and strike Rubén Silva on the head with a wooden bat. Neither did she see Rubén fall to the floor. The big man sat down on the edge of the bed and took Larissa in his arms. While he rocked her, he looked into her face, called her his beautiful brown-eyed girl, and calmed her. And while he did this, Larissa felt his warm tears washing over her swollen and bloody face.

"Braulio, Braulio, thank goodness you've come," Larissa whispered.

After Braulio laid Larissa on the bed, he went through the pockets of the unconscious Rubén Silva. Finding the key, he quickly unlocked the handcuffs. King Carlos came out from under the bed and jumped up beside Larissa. She cuddled him as she softly cried and wondered why her world had gone crazy.

The police soon arrived, as did an ambulance that took Larissa to the hospital where Mimi was waiting for her. The older woman fretted and worried while a doctor treated Larissa for the damages to her body that Rubén Silva had inflicted. Mimi stayed all night at the hospital, but Larissa did not know this because she had been given a strong sedative which put her into a deep sleep.

Early the next morning, Larissa awoke in her dimly lit hospital room and found she was looking into the face of a young woman standing beside her bed.

"I'm Madeline Wolf, Aaron's sister. How do you feel?" The woman put her hand gently on Larissa's arm.

"I think I'm okay." Larissa tried to smile.

"I'm glad I was able to get help to you. It was smart of you not to hang up the phone." The woman patted Larissa's hand.

"What phone?" Larissa was confused.

149

"When you called me looking for Aaron last night, I heard almost everything that happened to you because you didn't hang up your telephone receiver. I knew I had to get you help."

"I think I just dropped it." Larissa could not remember for sure about the telephone.

"Well, I went to my nearest neighbor and called La Llorona Cantina because Aaron had said he was going there to meet you. Aaron wasn't there yet, but I talked to a man, and I told him what you had said. The man assured me he would call the police." Madeline Wolf stopped talking for a moment, and then lowered her voice. "I went back home and listened to you on my telephone. It must have been horrible for you."

Neither woman talked for several moments.

Finally, Larissa said, "I don't know why Aaron never told me you lived with him."

Madeline smiled. "Well, he should have told you, but Aaron can be strange, and he doesn't disclose a lot about himself. Some people don't even know he has two sisters."

Larissa looked into the young woman's eyes. "I love your brother very much."

"And I know he feels the same about you," Madeline said.

Larissa did not see Aaron who was standing just inside the doorway. Neither did she see him lower his head, turn, and walk out of her room. Larissa did not see this because her eyes were closed as she wept in the arms of Madeline Wolf.

Chapter Fourteen

The doctor had insisted on Larissa staying home from work for a week after the attack by Rubén Silva. Mimi came by to see Larissa every day. On the last day of her convalescence, Mimi visited Larissa for just a short while, but long enough to let Larissa know she had some concerns about her.

"Are you sure you're ready to go back to work? You've been brutally terrorized."

"I need to get back to the museum, and as long as Rubén Silva stays away from me, I'm not afraid." Larissa stretched out on the sofa.

"Well, I think Rubén Silva wouldn't want any more trouble than what he's already got. I hope the district attorney follows through on his promise of charging that crazy man with the most serious charges possible." Mimi covered Larissa's feet with the afghan which lay on the end of the sofa. "I'm also worried about your love affair with Aaron. You and he may find it difficult to go back to the way things were."

"Why do you say such a thing? Why should we find it difficult?" Larissa felt a little alarmed.

Mimi picked up her purse from the lamp table. "Because of Trixie Trujillo and Rubén Silva, the two of you have had a serious and stressful disruption in your relationship."

Larissa smiled at Mimi. "Aaron and I just need some time together."

"I'm pleased with the way you've quickly recovered. Your eyes look normal again and the cuts are quickly healing, however I'm a little concerned about your emotional health."

"I'm getting back to normal. Carmelita has given me gallons of special teas." Larissa feigned a gagging response. "And she guarantees that her cures should do wonders for my emotions and everything else that's wrong with me."

"Well, you've been through a terrible trauma." Mimi headed toward the door. "I need to get back to the cantina before the evening crowd overwhelms Braulio." Mimi opened the front door. "It looks like you've got company, Larissa."

Aaron greeted Mimi as she walked out of the house and he walked in. He did not say anything to Larissa as he walked over to the sofa and stood looking down at her.

"Sit down." Larissa pointed to the end of the sofa.

"No. I want to stand here and look at you," Aaron said.

Larissa sat up. "I can't get accustomed to my short hair." She ran both of her hands through her hair. "I'm afraid you won't like it so short."

Aaron smiled at her. "I like your hair short." He hesitated. "And I also like it long." He put his hand on the top of her head and patted her. "Either way, I like it."

She did not respond but took his hand and held his palm against her lips.

He quietly said, "I'm sorry I didn't bring you a rose today. I didn't take the time to go buy one because I was in a hurry to see you."

"You've brought me enough flowers. Save your money. I just want you to sit down beside me."

Aaron sat down. "Where is Carmelita? Isn't she still staying with you?"

"Yes, but she went home to cook something for her husband. She'll be back in just a little while. She refuses to leave me here alone at night."

"I'm glad she's staying with you." Aaron picked up Larissa's hand and held it. "Larissa, I need to tell you I feel guilty, and I blame myself for what Rubén Silva did to you." He hesitated and took a deep breath. "I've been thinking. I should have told you about Madeline. I should have introduced you to her. That way you would have known Silva was lying."

"You shouldn't feel bad about that." She squeezed his hand. "He was just trying to get you out of the picture."

"But it's still my fault, because you never would have met Rubén Silva if I hadn't left the cantina with that woman." Aaron looked down. "I had no idea she was a prostitute."

"Why in the world did you walk out of the cantina with Trixie?"

Aaron raised his head and looked at Larissa. "She asked me to, and she said she was a friend of yours. I guess I was lashing out at you because of Victor Galván. I was very angry at you and jealous when I saw him kiss you."

Larissa shook her head. "That's not a rational excuse." She pulled her hand away from his grasp and looked away.

"I wasn't rational. I had drunk too much beer." He put his hand on Larissa's cheek and turned her face toward him. "Larissa, I'm sorry. Please forgive me."

"I forgive you, and I want to tell you again how sorry I am to have thought you had wives and children. Please forgive me."

"It's okay. I realize Silva tricked you. As long as you know who Madeline and Rosa really are, that's all that matters." Aaron put his arm around Larissa and pulled her closer to him.

He had explained to Larissa, several times during the past week, about his obligations to his sisters. Madeline's husband had been killed, and Aaron had agreed to support her and her children while she took classes in accounting. Aaron's sister Rosa also needed financial help because her husband was in prison.

Larissa pulled back from Aaron and looked intently at him. "You can't imagine how stupid and angry I felt when Rubén told me you had a wife and an ex-wife. And now I'm angry at myself because I should have known better. Eloy would have already told me about your marriages if it had been true. Don't you think he would have?"

"Yes, he probably would have told you."

They sat without talking for a while, he gently stroking her face with his finger tips, and she enjoying his touch.

Larissa broke the silence. "Carmelita made a coconut cream pie. Do you want some?"

"No, I don't have time because I have a department meeting in a few minutes." He seemed to be disappointed.

Larissa took Aaron's hand and held it. "I want to ask you a favor. Please, will you take me up to El Perico Mesa? I feel a need to go, to renew my spirit."

He hesitated a moment. "Yes, I'll take you, but I can't go until Sunday. We can leave early." He gently touched his lips to hers, and then he arose and walked to the door. "I'm glad you're better." He smiled at her just before he walked out.

* * *

On Sunday, Larissa got up before daybreak and made ham and cheese sandwiches and boiled eggs. She packed the lunch in a small ice chest and filled her canteen with water. It was late spring, and she knew that the higher country could be cold and even get snow at this time of the year. She put a wool blanket inside of her sleeping bag, rolled up the bag, and added it to the items to take. By the time she had things ready to go, Aaron arrived to get her.

She liked riding with him in the cab of his pickup. It gave her a sense of being close to him. He always seemed to like it when she sat next to him in the cab because he would smile a lot at her and occasionally reach over and pat her leg.

On the way to El Perico Mesa, Aaron laid his hand on her knee and said, "Tell me the truth. Are you feeling your normal self again?"

"Yes, I feel fine physically." Larissa sighed. "But I'm a little concerned about our relationship.

Mimi says we may have problems returning to the way we were before Rubén Silva."

Aaron hesitated a moment. "Well, I don't understand why we should have problems."

"Because of what's happened. What we've done and said to one another, I guess."

"Well, Larissa, I think we have already forgiven one another. Let's forget the bad things and put them behind us."

"But I've heard you say when we don't remember our past, we are doomed to repeat it. Isn't that right?"

Aaron laughed. "I think what I meant is if we don't learn from the errors of our past, then we will most likely repeat them."

"Tell me, Aaron. What have you learned from your errors?"

He chuckled. "That's easy. Not to drink too much beer and to first make sure a woman is not a prostitute before I walk outside with her."

Larissa tried to laugh, but it just would not come out. "I talked badly to you on the telephone, and I went out to dinner with Rubén Silva, and I even let him kiss me. Now, I'm wondering if you really want to be intimate with me again."

"Don't be ridiculous, Larissa." Aaron turned his head and looked at her and the pickup swerved.

"Watch the road, please." She took his hand from her knee and placed it back on the steering wheel, and then she moved closer to him and put her arm around his shoulders.

He laughed. "If I didn't want an intimate relationship with you, I'd have to be crazy!"

She kissed him on the cheek and sat with her arm around him all the rest of the way to El Perico Mesa.

Upon arriving on top of the mesa, Aaron parked his vehicle just off the road in a stand of pine trees. There had been little traffic on the highway from Los Espíritus. Coming up the dirt road leading to the mesa, Aaron had remarked how it appeared no vehicles had passed recently. Because the mesa was deserted, Larissa had the feeling it belonged to her and Aaron and to no one else.

After getting out of the pickup, they walked into the shadows of the trees toward the northwest. The air felt cool and a breeze moved silently through the boughs of the pines. Aaron took Larissa's hand and led her across the clearing to the edge of the mesa where they stood looking down at the tent rocks.

"Aaron, do you remember what you called these formations the first time you and I stood here together?" Larissa wondered if he would even remember the conversation from their first meeting.

"Yes, I called them the village of the tribe of giants. And I remember you with your braids up under a dirty hat. You looked like a little boy." He put his arm around her shoulders.

"I don't know why I find this place so enchanting, but I think it has to do with meeting you here." Larissa turned and, encircling his waist with her arms, laid her cheek against his chest and closed her eyes.

"I have something for you," he whispered.

157

"What is it?" She stepped back and stood looking at him.

"It's in my pocket." He unsnapped the button on the left pocket of his shirt and took out a sterling silver ring with a heart-shaped turquoise stone. "I had it made for you." He held it out so she could see it. "You can wear it on your right hand, but if you ever fall in love with me, you should move it to the left hand. That way I'll know." He took her right hand and put the ring on her finger.

Larissa did not speak. She just looked at Aaron, looked down at the ring, and then looked back at Aaron. She slowly removed the ring from her right hand and put it on the ring finger of her left hand. As she did this, he watched. He was smiling at her. Then they stood for a long time holding one another.

Larissa finally said, "Don't you want me to tell you that I love you, or is seeing the ring on my left hand enough for you?"

"I want to hear you say it."

"Aaron, I love you."

She waited to see if he would say anything, but he did not. "Well, is there anything you want to tell me?" She stepped back from him.

"Yes, and I'll tell the whole world." He turned toward the tent rocks, cupped his hands around his mouth, and yelled, "I love this woman!" His words rang out over the tent rocks, and down to the valley, and along the winding river, and across to the higher mountains.

Larissa put her hand on Aaron's arm. "Thank you for telling the whole world, and when you're ready to tell me, you know where you can find me." She laughed and started to walk away.

He caught her arm and pulled her back to him and whispered in her ear, "I love you, Larissa, and I should have been telling you this everyday for a long, long time."

They started to leave, but Larissa stopped and looked down at the tent rocks. "I feel a connection with this place. My spirit is full of joy when I am here." She moved closer to him and whispered, "And my spirit is happiest when you are here with me."

He held her tightly and said, "My spirit is happy to be with you, but right now my stomach is unhappy and growling." Then he laughed.

She pushed him away from her. "Okay, do you want to eat a sandwich?"

They walked back to his pickup and she got out the lunch. He lowered the tailgate and they sat on it to eat. Just as they were finishing their meal, two Stellar jays began making loud raucous noises in a pine tree not far from the pickup. The birds seemed to be having a loud lover's quarrel as they flew from branch to branch.

"I think he's courting her," Aaron said.

"Maybe she's courting him. You can't tell which one is which." Larissa laughed.

"You're right. I just hope he enjoys making love to her as much as I enjoy making love to you." He smiled broadly at Larissa.

She began putting things away. "Did you know Stellar jays mate for life? They are monogamous."

"I didn't know that," Aaron said and arranged a few items in the bed of the pickup.

"I wish you and I could be like the jays." She spoke these words in the relaxed manner which she used quite often with him.

Aaron dropped what he had in his hand and quickly turned toward her. "I'd be happy for us to be like the jays. I want an exclusive relationship with you; in fact, I'd like for us to think about something permanent. And that's something else I should have been telling you for a long, long time."

Larissa moved closer to Aaron. "I wasn't sure how you felt—you've told me you have too many obligations for anything serious, and I can see you certainly do."

Aaron closed the tailgate of the pickup. "Things are going to get better. My sisters won't need my financial help much longer."

Then Aaron turned to Larissa and put his hands on her shoulders. "And there's something I haven't told you. I've applied for a position with the Department of the Interior. If I get hired, I can make a lot more money than what I'm making teaching at the College."

Larissa had not considered the idea of Aaron leaving Santa Elena College. Now, she supposed he most likely would have to move to Santa Fe or Albuquerque if he got a job with the federal government. This would not be ideal, but it would be all right. She would face this when the time came.

"So, Aaron, are you saying something permanent would be—you know—marriage?"

"Yes, that's precisely what I'm saying—precisely what I'm asking you."

Larissa said nothing more, but reached into the bed of Aaron's pickup and pulled her sleeping bag out. She looked at Aaron and smiled, then pointed to the sleeping bag. Aaron took the bag from her and led her to a large fir where he laid out the sleeping bag under a low lying branch.

While Larissa and Aaron stayed in the sleeping bag most of the afternoon making love, the Stellar jays made loud noises as they chased one another among the pines. Larissa did not hear the noisy birds because she heard only words of love being whispered in her ear by Aaron Wolf.

Chapter Fifteen

Aaron had not been hired by the College to teach classes during the summer. For this reason he took a temporary job in Oklahoma.

"I can't make it financially without working in the summer, otherwise I wouldn't leave you," he had told Larissa.

"When will you be back?" The thought of him leaving upset her.

"I'll be back in late August in time for the beginning of the fall semester, unless in the meantime I get a position with the Department of the Interior. That will change everything."

Larissa told him she did not know how she could go so long without seeing him. He promised, if he could, he would come and spend the Fourth of July with her.

To help ease the pain of Aaron's absence, Larissa threw herself wholeheartedly into the summer session at the College. Besides working in the museum, she taught a class of advanced anthropology. It was while teaching this class that she overheard some of her students whispering about Eloy and the inappropriate things he had supposedly done to some of the young women at the College. Larissa did not hesitate to ask all of the female students to stay a few minutes at the end of class.

Standing before the group of twelve young women, Larissa said, "I have overheard some of you saying things about Dr. Flores which leads me

163

to think he is doing some things he shouldn't be doing. Is it true?"

No one responded.

Larissa looked around the room into the face of each young woman. She continued. "I want you ladies to know something. Dr. Flores has been inappropriate with me. He has made sexual remarks to me and has touched me on parts of my body which are off limits. I've reported this, but nothing has been done." Larissa stopped talking for a few moments and then cleared her throat. "If Dr. Flores is doing the same to any of you, I need you to come forth and let me know so we can join forces against him. If any of you have something to tell me, call me at my office, or just stay here for a few more minutes." Larissa sat down at her classroom desk.

Five of the students stayed behind. They sat, not moving and all looking attentively at Larissa.

"Would you be willing to reveal what Dr. Flores has done to you?" Larissa asked the students.

Most seemed a little hesitant, but one said she would be glad to do it. The other four said they probably would as long as it did not hurt their grades.

One of the students said, "We call Dr. Flores 'the handy man' because he can't keep his hands to himself. And I'll tell you the truth, Dr. Lozoya. I know he has sexually harassed two of the students who didn't stay to talk to you today. Everybody's afraid of retaliation."

Another young woman said, "I dread to think of what my parents and my brothers are going to think if this goes public. They won't like it."

"I understand, but aren't you tired of being afraid to report a man like Eloy Flores? I think it's time women take control of their lives and their bodies." Larissa stood up. "Feel free to call me, either at my office or at home. I'm in the telephone directory."

After the students left, Larissa went straight to Pete Ríos's office. He listened to her while she told him what had just transpired in her classroom.

As he slowly shook his head, he said, "I'm sorry, Larissa. I didn't realize how serious it was. I thought there was something romantic between you and Eloy. But if Eloy is abusing any of our female students, then something will have to be done. I'll contact the Dean and you write up the report from today's meeting with your students. I will investigate this—even if it means a disruption in Eloy's summer work at El Perico Mesa."

"Thank you Dr. Ríos. And, by the way, I made a police report several months ago about an incident that happened in my office. I called you at home about it. I've also decided I want to talk to an attorney, so I can take civil action against Eloy and the College if something isn't done to remove Eloy." Larissa looked at Pete Ríos with a serious expression on her face.

He responded with an equally serious look. "Trust me, Larissa, something will be done, but it will take time. Eloy Flores has tenure, and he has rights. Don't forget that."

* * *

Larissa had not forgotten it would take time to get rid of Eloy, but the days seemed to be passing too slowly for her. Almost four weeks of the summer session had gone by, and she had heard rumors that Pete Ríos was carrying out an investigation of the charges made by Larissa. But she had heard nothing from Pete Ríos regarding the situation. Neither had she received notification of the department's summer field work plans. Eloy and his student assistants should have already been working at one of the archeological dig sites for the summer, but they weren't. Because of this, Larissa suspected something might be happening with Eloy. She just did not know for sure what.

One morning on campus when she saw José García, Eloy's student assistant, Larissa asked him about the summer plans.

"I don't know for sure what's going on, but everything's on hold for some reason. Dr. Flores may not be free to leave, and that means I won't have any summer income from the student work program. I hope I can find another job." José seemed worried.

This conversation with José gave Larissa new hope. Perhaps, at last, the College was investigating Eloy.

Later the same day, while Larissa was working at her desk in her office, a woman suddenly walked in, stopped, and put her hands on her hips.

"Are you Larissa Lozoya?" The chubby, bleached blonde asked.

The woman annoyed Larissa because she had barged in without knocking.

166

"Yes. What can I do for you?" Larissa asked.

"I want to warn you, if you don't quit persecuting my husband, you will be extremely sorry!" Spittle spewed out of the woman's mouth as she yelled these words at Larissa.

"Who are you?" Larissa arose from her chair and looked curiously across her desk at the woman who stood on the other side.

The woman shook her finger vigorously at Larissa. "I'm Epifania Flores, Dr. Flores's wife! That's who I am! And I'm the woman who is going to make your life miserable if you don't withdraw your complaints against my husband and say you were lying about him!"

"Mrs. Flores, I'm sorry to tell you, but your husband has done everything I've accused him of. He has grabbed me and rubbed his body all over me right here in this office." Larissa pointed to the spot where Eloy had pushed her up against the wall.

"Lies! All lies! You're a liar! You've even turned his students against him. You're just angry because you've wanted to have an affair with my husband and he refused you!" Epifania Flores stomped her foot. "And my husband told me you're always putting your hands all over him and trying to get him to kiss you."

Larissa picked up the telephone receiver and called for campus security.

The obviously irate Epifania turned and walked out of the office, but returned to the doorway just long enough to say in a very loud voice, "I will get you for this, you slut! You'll be sorry you ever heard of Eloy and Epifania Flores!"

Eloy's wife had left campus by the time the security officer arrived. Epifania Flores's outburst had taken Larissa by surprise, and she wondered why Epifania had suggested Larissa wanted a relationship with Eloy. Perhaps Eloy had told his wife this to defend a position of innocence. Maybe if the female students would testify, and four of them had said they would, Epifania Flores might eventually formulate a different opinion of her husband.

Larissa told herself not to get too upset about Epifania Flores and her ugly tirade. The woman must be crazy, and no one would believe the stupid things she had said anyway. Besides, Larissa did not have time to worry about Epifania Flores because there were many tasks to complete in the museum, and teaching the anthropology class required a lot of preparation. Keeping herself busy helped Larissa to cope with life without Aaron, and she looked forward to Aaron's promised visit. In fact, she counted the days until his expected arrival. But she did not have to wait until Independence Day to see Aaron because he unexpectedly showed up at her house a few days earlier than planned.

When she opened the door and saw him, she cried out "Aaron, I'm so happy you're here!" Then she threw her arms around him. The elation of seeing Aaron overcame Larissa, and she started crying and kissing him at the same time.

Aaron held her tightly in his arms and whispered, "I missed you too much, and I wanted to be with you. I asked for two extra days off from work."

They spent all three days of Aaron's visit without going out of the house, and Larissa told Carmelita to take a little vacation. Larissa thoroughly enjoyed having Aaron all to herself. They made love, they ate tuna fish sandwiches, they drank lots of coffee, and they talked for hours. Aaron said Madeline had moved to Tulsa and had a very good job, and Rosa was expecting her husband to be paroled soon. Larissa told Aaron about her work in the museum, but she did not mention Epifania Flores's unwelcomed visit.

Aaron left on the Fourth of July. The drive back to central Oklahoma was long, and he had to return to his job the next day. Larissa tried to work the day after Aaron left but, as soon as her class was over, she went home and went to bed.

"You're too much in love, *m'ija*," said Carmelita. "Let me prepare you a special tea."

Larissa drank Carmelita's tea, but it just gave her diarrhea and made her feel worse than she already did.

"Let me prepare you something for the diarrhea," said Carmelita.

And so it went, Carmelita tried to alleviate Larissa's melancholy with her special brews of herbs and teas, but nothing seemed to alter how Larissa felt about missing Aaron. He telephoned her every Sunday evening, and when she hung up the telephone receiver, she usually went to bed and cried herself to sleep.

* * *

One morning in late August as Larissa was sitting at the desk in her office, Pete Ríos walked in. "Larissa, I'm sorry to tell you, but unless you can provide proof of Eloy's mistreatment of you, there's really nothing the College can do about your accusations."

Larissa was taken aback. "What kind of proof? I have no witnesses. And what about the female students I told you about?"

Pete cleared his throat. "Well, there have been no reports from any female students."

Larissa frowned. "There may have been no reports yet, but they will testify when there's a hearing for Eloy. I'm almost certain of that."

Pete shrugged his shoulders. "Well, Larissa, I've investigated your complaint thoroughly, and until you can give me something substantial to go on, there's nothing more I can do. I wish you could just take care of this problem yourself—rapidly and discreetly." He looked at Larissa and gave her a quick smile. "I'm worried that you're going to get yourself in lots of hot water with the upper echelon. I sure would hate to lose you." With that, Pete Ríos turned and walked out of Larissa's office without closing the door.

Larissa came up out of her chair with the intention of trying to stop Pete so she could attempt to discuss the issue more, but she got no farther than the doorway and stopped. One of the female students who had complained about Eloy was approaching. Larissa could tell by her appearance she had been crying.

"What's wrong?" Larissa asked when the young woman stepped into her office.

"Well, I'm really sorry, but I can't testify against Dr. Flores. None of us can." The student dropped her head and looked down at the floor.

Larissa walked over to her desk, sat down, took a deep breath, and let it out. "Why not?"

"Because we've all been threatened with failure and termination if we say anymore about Dr. Flores." The student slowly shook her head. "My father was even called by someone—wouldn't give their name—said I was causing lots of trouble here and my father better talk some sense into me."

"I'm sorry to hear this," Larissa said.

"I need to go, Dr. Lasoya. I have a class." The student moved toward the doorway. "And please believe me—I'm truly, truly sorry."

Larissa sat unmoving and staring into space for a good while after the student had disappeared through the doorway. How could this possibly be happening? Larissa was being made the culprit, not Eloy; Larissa had been told by Pete Ríos *she* needed to rectify the problem; although she had provided Pete with the names of other victims of Eloy, it did not seem to matter; and Epifania Flores had accused Larissa of doing things with Eloy that made Larissa gag just thinking about it.

Now as Larissa sat mulling over the sad turn of events, she decided she would do what any good American would do—she would sue Eloy Flores, Pete Ríos, Epifania Flores, the Dean and President of the College, and the College itself. Yes, she would show all of these people they cannot deny her justice. Larissa had the right to "life, liberty, and the pursuit of happiness" and her happiness was seriously being curtailed. Larissa cleared her desk and walked out of her office. She hummed a happy tune all the way home.

Chapter Sixteen

Larissa waited at home all afternoon for Aaron. He had telephoned her earlier to say he had arrived in Los Espíritus and would see her just as soon as he had finished some business at the College. She eagerly wanted to see him, put her arms around him, and tell him she loved him.

It was just before dark when Aaron knocked on Larissa's front door. She could not restrain her excitement and rushed to the door and opened it. "Aaron, I'm so happy to see you! My goodness, how much I've missed you!" She smiled and motioned for him to come in.

He did not speak, and she immediately sensed something must be wrong by the unusual look on his face. He was not smiling as he always did when she met him at the door.

He stepped into the living room and abruptly stopped. "Well, don't you have something you need to tell me?"

His question surprised Larissa.

"I certainly do have something to tell you—I love you." She smiled at him and held her arms open, but he stepped back from her.

He did not show any apparent pleasure at seeing her. "Oh, so you love me? Well, you don't really expect me to believe that, do you?" He glared at Larissa.

"Aaron, what's wrong with you?" Larissa's face began to flush, and her stomach felt a bit queasy.

"I'll tell you what's wrong with me. I can't even be gone a couple of months without you hooking up with Eloy." Aaron gave Larissa a nasty look.

"That's not true! How can you say such a terrible thing?" Larissa began having problems breathing.

"Epifania Flores told me what you have done. I saw her at the College when I went to my office this afternoon. She told me all about you and Eloy."

"Aaron! You already know I can't tolerate him." Larissa began to tremble.

Aaron narrowed his eyes. "Epifania told me she suspected for a long time that you and Eloy have been having sex every chance you can get. And now she has caught you."

Larissa gasped. "Caught us! That's not true!" She sat down on the end of the sofa. "It never happened, Aaron. I swear to you—it never happened!" Tears began running down Larissa's face.

"Epifania said she walked in on the two of you in your office. She said you were definitely having sex on your little settee!" Aaron's voice had progressively gotten louder and his chin now slightly quivered.

"Aaron, calm down and please listen to me. I have filed numerous formal complaints against Eloy and even a police report because he came into my office, grabbed me, and rubbed himself all over me." Larissa wiped the tears from her face with her hand and took a deep breath. "Epifania Flores came to my office and threatened me. She said I'd be sorry if I didn't recant my story and withdraw the complaints against Eloy. Now look what she's done."

Aaron pointed his finger at Larissa. "I don't believe you. You never told me anything about Eloy coming in to your office and grabbing you. And why hadn't you told me about Epifania threatening you?" Aaron hesitated and shook his head. "I've telephoned you every week and you have never mentioned Epifania."

"I just didn't want to bother you with it because you weren't here, and you couldn't have done anything about it anyway. And, besides, I always wanted to talk to you about other things. Aaron, it's true. Eloy's wife did threaten me."

Aaron shook his finger at Larissa. "That sounds fabricated, Larissa. Epifania warned me you'd say something like this to try to convince me you're innocent."

"Aaron, she's lying!" Larissa began sobbing.

"Why would a wife tell something so terribly embarrassing about her own husband if it wasn't true? And Eloy has made some hints about you which I didn't like. I just never told you." Aaron looked angrily at Larissa. "I don't know why you have done me this way. You've whored yourself, and I want nothing more to do with you." Aaron turned away from her.

Larissa stood and reached out to Aaron. "Wait! Let's talk about this."

"I have nothing more to say to you." He turned and opened the door.

Larissa rushed to him and grabbed one of his arms with both of her hands. "Aaron, don't leave me! Please, I love you!" She continued to hold on to his arm.

He tried to pull away from her.

"Aaron, don't be a fool!" Larissa tightened her hold.

Aaron shook his head, grimaced, and said, "You shouldn't have been a whore! I don't love you!" He pulled himself free of her and walked out of the house, slamming the door behind him.

Larissa stumbled backwards and fell painfully upon Brother Bear. The tears came pouring from her, and she cried as she had never cried before. King Carlos came into the living room and sat down and looked at her. As Larissa cried, a horrible feeling of hopelessness welled up inside of her. She felt abandoned and desperate.

Larissa arose, stopped crying and went to her bedroom. She telephoned Mimi and told her about the scene she had just had with Aaron.

"Oh, give him time, sweetie. He's like a lot of men. They run off at the mouth before they bother to use their brains." Mimi laughed.

"No, Mimi, it's not that simple. He honestly believes all of this has happened." Larissa began to cry. "I don't think Aaron will ever be back. He called me a whore and said he didn't love me, and he wanted no more to do with me."

"Larissa, he's just angry, and he's been given too much information to process at one time.

Wait and see." Mimi seemed to be trying to reassure Larissa. "But I must admit his reaction does surprise me."

"Everything he said and did today surprises me. I never thought he would do anything like this." Larissa hesitated a moment. "Mimi, I think I'll go see my lawyer and sue Eloy and Epifania—and the College."

Mimi gasped. "I don't know if you'd get anywhere with a lawsuit. Wouldn't you have to prove that you were libeled or slandered or something like that?"

"I don't know what I'd have to prove. The most important thing is for Aaron to believe I've told the truth. I guess Mr. Montes will have to determine all of that for me but I . . . ."

Mimi broke in, "Oh, Larissa, you silly girl. You're not actually thinking of using Willy Montes as your lawyer. Don't you know he's a member of the good old boys club?"

"Well, yes I would use him. He's the only lawyer I've ever used."

"Yes, but for deeds, and trusts, and wills. You can't use him for this. He's a good friend of Pete Ríos and Eloy Flores, not to mention all the other old boys at the College."

"So you're saying I have no recourse, I have no way of getting Aaron back."

Mimi took a big breath and let it out. "First of all, I'm saying you don't need to work at the College. You don't need to work at all. And as far as Aaron—well, I don't know what to say."

Larissa began crying uncontrollably, and she did not respond to Mimi. Finally, Larissa hung up the telephone receiver. Nothing about her life felt real anymore except the desperation and hopelessness which were overwhelming her.

She went into the kitchen and slowly took a pill bottle from the cupboard. Opening the bottle, she saw she still had some of the pain pills given to her by her dentist when she had had two wisdom teeth extracted. Taking the bottle with her, Larissa went into her father's den where she lay down on the four-poster bed and let her body sink down into the consoling softness of the feathers. She wondered if there were enough pills to actually kill her. Perhaps she would pass out before she could ingest a lethal dose. Then she thought of Aaron. If she died, he would lose the woman who loved him and had been faithful to him. Surely he would eventually learn the truth. That would hurt him, and she wanted him to feel as much pain as she was feeling now. But, more than anything, she wanted to end the horrible agony which seemed to be killing her spirit. She poured all of the pills into her hand.

Suddenly, King Carlos jumped up onto the bed and then onto Larissa's abdomen, knocking the breath from her lungs and the pills from her hand. Then he quickly leapt off the bed, leaving Larissa gasping. While she was gathering the pills, the telephone rang. Larissa thought it might be Aaron calling to tell her again he did not love her. She returned the pills to the bottle, arose from the bed, and answered the phone.

It was Mimi. "Okay, if you're really serious about this, I know a lawyer whom I trust. She might be able to get something done for you." Mimi sounded calm and reassuring.

"Oh, thank goodness. Where?" Larissa felt relieved.

"In Albuquerque, that's where. Her name's Kitty Cohen and she's a real witch when it comes to suing men. I've known her for years."

Larissa laughed. "Oh, Mimi, thank you. Can you take me to her? When can we go?"

"Just hang on. I'll have to call first to see if I can get it set up for tomorrow." Mimi sounded rather reluctant. "And remember this, Larissa. If you sue, you'll be exposing all your dirty laundry for everyone to see. That may be difficult for you."

"I don't care how difficult it is. I just want to punish Eloy and his wife, and, most of all, I want Aaron to find out the truth and regret what he said to me today."

"Well, Larissa, I hope you're not the one who will regret all of this. Anyway, we'll leave early in the morning if I can arrange it for tomorrow. I'll call Kitty, and I'll tell her the whole sordid story."

* * *

At eight-thirty the next morning, Aaron came to Larissa's house, but Larissa was not aware of it. He knocked and knocked on the front door; no one answered. Neither did Larissa see Aaron go around to the back door and knock, nor did she notice him look into her garage before he went again to the back door. Larissa did not witness any of this because she and Mimi were traveling south down the highway at seventy miles per hour in Mimi's old, baby-blue Buick Roadmaster.

It was shortly after noon when the two women arrived in Albuquerque. Mimi quickly found Kitty Cohen's small office. It was in an old strip mall on East Central Avenue across from the fair grounds. Kitty, a tiny woman with thick makeup and dyed black hair, appeared cordial and ushered Mimi and Larissa into her office.

After seating the two women, Kitty looked at Larissa with a slight smile on her face. "So you want to sue your employer and a good-for-nothing colleague. How marvelous!"

Larissa smiled back and nodded her head.

"Well, first of all . . . ," Kitty said and cleared her throat. "Do you have a hundred-thousand dollars to give me up front? This will be an expensive suit if you want to sue everyone that Mimi told me you wanted to sue. So it'll take about a hundred thousand."

Larissa was stunned. "Well, no I really don't have . . . maybe I could sell something." Larissa slumped back in her chair.

Kitty continued, "Tell me this. How many witnesses do you have? I mean that actually saw and heard what your colleague did to you?"

"None." Alyssa looked down and then suddenly sat straight up in her chair. "But I have several students who have had the same problem with the same man."

"And they're willing to testify?" Kitty looked at Larissa with unblinking eyes.

180

Larissa slumped down again. "Probably not. They've been threatened."

"And you? Have you been threatened?" Kitty asked.

"Not really. I mean—not in so many words" Larissa took in a big breath and blew it out. "But I swear to you, Miss Cohen, Eloy Flores has bothered me for two years. He has grabbed me and rubbed his body all over me, and now—now his stupid wife is telling people I'm involved in a sexual relationship with Eloy. It's just not true." Larissa began to cry.

Kitty stood up. "Larissa, stop crying and listen to me. Until our government gets off its butt and passes some laws that protect women from sexual harassment in the work place, there's not much we can do in the courts in this kind of case."

Mimi spoke up, "Well, that's too bad then. I think Larissa just needs to quit her job at that college. She doesn't have to put up with that crap from those blasted men!"

Larissa turned toward Mimi. "I don't want to quit my job. I still lack one more year developing the museum—and I love the work." Larissa began sobbing again.

Kitty walked over to Larissa and laid her hand on Larissa's shoulder. "I'm sorry, but without witnesses it's just your word against Eloy Flores's. And I understand, from what Mimi has told me, Eloy has tenure and you're just a rookie. So, you don't have much of a chance. It would take something like charges of moral turpitude to get rid of this Eloy character."

Larissa quit crying and looked up at Kitty. "Moral turpitude? Like what?"

"Oh, like exposing himself to several people—or better yet, running naked all over the campus." Kitty laughed and patted Larissa on the back.

Later that evening, a dejected Larissa got back into the Buick Roadmaster, and she and Mimi started north for Los Espíritus. Because of her disappointment with the outcome of her meeting with Kitty Cohen, Larissa talked very little, but occasionally she would say something about how much she hated Aaron Wolf and then she would cry.

Mimi finally said, "Quit saying you hate Aaron. I know you don't hate him, because you're still madly in love with him."

"I know I am, but, oh how I wish I hated him."

"Well, try thinking about something else," Mimi said as she pressed her foot down hard on the accelerator

Larissa did what Mimi told her to do—she began thinking about something else. She thought about what Kitty Cohen had said regarding Eloy and moral turpitude. In fact, Larissa thought a great deal about it.

Shortly after dark, Mimi delivered Larissa back to her house and said she would stay overnight if Larissa was too sad and upset to stay alone. Larissa insisted she was fine. After Mimi left, Larissa busied herself putting things away. When she went into the kitchen to turn out the lights, King

Carlos meowed loudly and sat down next to his empty food bowl.

"You poor cat," Larissa said. "Didn't Carmelita feed you anything while I was gone?"

Larissa poured dried food into his bowl. While looking in the cupboard for a can of tuna fish, Larissa saw her bottle of pain pills. She took the bottle and put it in her pocket.

While Larissa was taking a shower, the telephone rang. She did not hear this because she was hearing only the water from the showerhead and the tune she was humming as she thought over and over about what Kitty Cohen had said regarding Eloy and moral turpitude.

Larissa had not been in bed more than half an hour when someone knocked on the front door. Maybe Larissa was not aware if this because she was deeply asleep as a result of having swallowed three of her pain pills. A few minutes later there came a knock on the backdoor. Perhaps Larissa did not hear it, but King Carlos raised his head and looked toward the hallway. When Larissa did not rouse, King Carlos curled up against Larissa's leg and went back to sleep, but was abruptly awakened when someone knocked on the bedroom window. It was possible that Larissa was not aware of this, but King Carlos clearly heard a familiar voice say, "Larissa, listen to me. I love you and I need to talk to you. Larissa, let me in. Please, Larissa, please."

Chapter Seventeen

"Do you want me to put a curse on that dirty *cabrona*?" Carmelita leaned against the kitchen table and looked down at Larissa who had just finished eating a bowl of Carmelita's delicious *fideo*. "I'll do it! Just get me some strands of that bleached blonde hair off the top of her filthy head. I'll make Epifania Flores sorry she ever mentioned your name to Aaron."

"Just calm down, I don't need you to do anything." Larissa handed her bowl to Carmelita and arose from the kitchen table. "I'm going to take care of her myself. But right now I have to go back to work."

It had been a week since Larissa had come back from Albuquerque, and she had had no contact with Aaron. Now with fall semester beginning, Larissa thought about how she would respond when she saw him on campus. She had not spent too much time thinking about Aaron, because Eloy Flores loomed foremost in her mind. Larissa now decided to take things into her own hands. Her only goal at the moment was to do something which would assuredly get Eloy dismissed from the College. He had been the cause of almost everything wrong in Larissa's life. If he had not sexually harassed her, she would not have filed complaints against him, and Eloy's wife would not have told Aaron the malicious lie which had caused her breakup with Aaron. Larissa now had a plan, and she needed to carry it out.

After brushing her teeth and combing her hair, Larissa went back into the kitchen. "Do you know where my red shawl is, the one with the long fringe?"

Carmelita wiped her hands on her apron. "Let me get it because you'll never find it."

Larissa reached down under the kitchen table and picked up her red Keds and put them on just as Carmelita returned with the shawl.

Carmelita frowned. "You don't need this shawl. It's warm outside."

"Well, you never know. I might need it in my office." Instead of putting it over her shoulders, Larissa put it under her arm.

As she took a new route across the campus, Larissa hummed a little tune. Needing to determine if Eloy Flores was in his office, she walked past the museum building and into the faculty office building. Except for a janitor who had just entered Aaron's office, she saw no one. As Larissa walked past the doorway to Aaron's office, she glanced in and noticed it appeared unusually uncluttered. She stopped and went back to the doorway. First, she saw the bare bookcases. Then she noticed Aaron's desk had nothing on it, and things which had been hanging on the walls were gone. Larissa stifled a gasp with the palm of her hand.

"Where's Dr. Wolf?" She looked at the janitor.

"He's gone—moved to Alaska." The janitor began sweeping.

This information shocked Larissa, and she found her breathing becoming difficult. She almost began crying while standing there in the hall. Just knowing Aaron was no longer in Los Espíritus saddened her deeply. She hated not having him in her life. He had hurt her, but she still loved him. She did not want to break down now; she wanted now more than ever to carry out her plan against Eloy. But first, Larissa needed to go to the history department and ask the secretary about Aaron.

The secretary stopped typing and looked up at Larissa. "Dr. Wolf resigned suddenly. He said he had applied a long time ago for a job with the Department of the Interior. I guess he heard something last week and he cleaned out his office and left yesterday." The secretary turned back to her typing.

Larissa then proceeded down the hall to see if Eloy's office door was open. She could hear him talking in his office. Smiling to herself, she turned and hurried out of the building and headed toward the museum.

To make sure her plan would work, Larissa placed a large wooden stick between the front door of the museum and the jamb. This would keep the door from closing and automatically locking. Then, she went into her office and quickly placed a small table along the wall under the window. Next, she raised the window about ten inches and went back to her desk. With Eloy Flores still in his office and Epifania Flores at home, Larissa had great hope of carrying out her scheme.

Smiling to herself, Larissa quickly telephoned Eloy's house. Epifania answered and, from the sound of her voice, Larissa thought she must have awakened the woman.

"Mrs. Flores, you don't know me, but I know your husband."

Larissa had lowered the pitch of her voice hoping the woman would not recognize it. After all, Epifania had heard Larissa's voice only once.

Larissa continued, "Your husband and Dr. Larissa Lozoya are having a hot affair right under your nose."

"What do you mean by hot affair?" Epifania seemed a little more awake.

"I mean sex, Mrs. Flores. You know sexual intercourse? They do it all the time." Larissa heard Epifania gasp. "If you go right now to Dr. Lazoya's office, you'll find them naked and having sex. I guarantee it. But be sure you go in through the front door of the museum, it's the only one that's unlocked."

Epifania Flores did not say thank you or good-bye, she just hung up the telephone. Larissa had only ten minutes, fifteen at most, to set the stage before Epifania Flores would arrive. Larissa quickly took off all of her clothing except for her red Keds. Then she took her shawl and wrapped it around her naked body.

After folding her skirt, blouse, and underwear, she placed these in the bottom drawer of her file cabinet. With her office door key, she unlocked the door and pushed the key down into the soil of one of the potted plants. This way no one could lock themselves into her office. Then she telephoned Eloy.

188

Larissa smiled broadly when she heard him answer, and sounding as sweet and as enticing as she could, she slowly said, "Eloy, can you come to my office. I really need to talk to you."

"What's up, *mi amor*?"

He called her his love again, but she no longer cared.

"Well, I was thinking, now that Aaron Wolf is out of the picture, maybe you and I could be a little friendlier. Will you come down to my office right now, please?"

"I'll be right there, *mi amor*."

Larissa unplugged her telephone and laid it on top of her clothing in the file drawer. She closed the drawer, locked it, and pushed the key down into the soil of another of her potted plants. Then, with the red shawl around her, she sat down on the settee to wait for Eloy. She did not have to wait very long because he almost immediately knocked on her office door. Before she could tell him to come in, he slowly opened the door and looked in.

"What do you need, *amorcita*?" He grinned at her.

"Please come in and close the door." Larissa smiled back at Eloy. "Take off your clothes. I've got something for you." Larissa forced herself to continue smiling as she lay back against the arm of the settee and beckoned to Eloy with her index finger.

He stared at her and did not move, so Larissa opened up the shawl and showed him her naked body.

"Hurry, Eloy. I took my clothes off for you. Now take your clothes off for me if you want to do it with me."

Eloy quickly walked through the doorway, closed the door behind him, and began taking off his shirt. As he removed each piece of clothing, Larissa neatly folded it and placed it on the table beneath the window. When she had finished this chore, she sat down on the settee and opened the shawl. Eloy stood a few feet in front of her, naked except for his feet which still had on shoes and socks. She looked at Eloy's face and saw long gray nose hairs protruding from his nostrils. They matched the hairs sticking out from his ear canals. *Poor Epifania*, Larissa thought, *why would she want this man?*

Larissa glanced at Eloy's penis, a flaccid thing, and about the size of one of those orange-colored candy peanuts that Braulio used to buy her when she was a child. Below Eloy's penis hung large, pendulous testicles. Larissa almost burst out laughing, but quickly regained her control. Eloy did not move. He just stood looking at Larissa with a somewhat quizzical look on his face.

"Well, Eloy. Is that all you've got? What am I supposed to do with such a little thing?" Larissa pointed to his penis. "Can't you even get an erection?" She stood up and pulled her shawl around her body and walked over to the window.

"Give me a chance," Eloy said. "I need a little time. You've surprised me. That's all."

"How do you like this surprise?" Larissa said as she picked up his clothing and threw everything out the window.

Eloy had already begun to masturbate with his eyes closed and did not seem to notice what Larissa had just done. "Please, *mi amor*. Just give me a chance." Eloy continued working on himself.

Larissa laughed, and as she turned, she pulled her shawl tightly around her body. She walked past Eloy and out of her office, closing the door behind her. Then she exited the back door of the museum and rushed into the faculty office building. Going into the first empty office she came to, she picked up the telephone receiver and called campus security.

"I need to report a crazy, naked man running around inside the anthropology museum building. Can you please send someone over quickly?"

She immediately hung up and rushed out to where Eloy's clothing was lying on the ground beneath her window. She picked up the bundle and carried it under her shawl as she proceeded down the sidewalk. Along the way she spotted a large trash can where she stopped and deposited Eloy's clothing. Holding the red shawl tightly with both hands, she continued on toward home.

Because Larissa was creating a new route home, one which went behind buildings, she did not observe Epifania Flores park her big red Cadillac in the faculty parking lot. Larissa did not see Epifania walk into the museum after picking up the stick which propped the front door open. Neither did Larissa notice Epifania open the door to Larissa's office where Epifania found her husband standing naked with his flaccid penis in his hand. Larissa could not have seen any of these things because she had quickly walked away from campus in nothing but her red shawl and her matching red Keds. She was humming a little tune.

Chapter Eighteen

Larissa opened the heavy front door and looked out. She thought she had heard a vehicle, but she saw nothing. King Carlos followed her to the door. Larissa opened the door wider so she could see if a vehicle had pulled into the driveway.

"Move back, King Carlos," she said as she pushed the cat away with the instep of her foot.

However, King Carlos quickly ran through the doorway and out into the yard.

"You naughty boy, get back in here!" Larissa yelled as she followed him into the yard.

He ran into the street and sat down. Being barefoot, Larissa proceeded cautiously across the front yard. Before she could reach King Carlos, he ran farther down the street and out of Larissa's sight behind a parked car.

"King Carlos, please . . . ." Larissa suddenly stopped because an automobile had come rapidly around the corner.

Larissa tightly closed her eyes as she heard the screeching of tires and then a loud thud. A bone-chilling shiver coursed through her body. On opening her eyes, she saw King Carlos lying in the middle of the street. The automobile failed to stop.

Larissa screamed and ran to her cat where she quickly scooped a lifeless King Carlos into her arms. The blood that was running from his mouth, ears, and rectum slowly found its way down the front of Larissa's blouse and dripped onto her bare feet. She held King Carlos to her breast and raising her face toward the sky, she screamed, "They killed my cat! Oh, God! Oh, God! They killed him!"

The automobile that had hit King Carlos backed up and stopped beside Larissa. A young man rolled down his window glass. "I'm really sorry, lady. I didn't see the cat."

Larissa stared at the driver and then said slowly and in a quiet voice, "Look what you've done, you murderer. You've killed King Carlos."

The young man laughed and said, "Get a grip, lady, it's just a cat." He then put the automobile's gear into low and sped off.

Larissa stood dumbfounded in the street. The autumn afternoon suddenly seemed unnaturally silent. She saw no vehicles moving, no people, nothing. Then she heard the baying of a dog somewhere in the distance. Its eerie wails sent shivers throughout Larissa's body. She thought of what she had given up in such a short time—first Aaron and now King Carlos. She wondered what more she would sacrifice

Larissa carried King Carlos into the house and placed him on the kitchen counter next to the sink. She put her ear against his body and heard nothing. His tongue lolled out of his mouth, and some of his urine ran out of his body and on to the counter top. He looked dead, and Larissa was certain he had no life left in him.

After cleaning him and then herself, she wrapped him in a towel and took him to lie with her on top of Brother Bear. Larissa cried herself to sleep, holding King Carlos against her body. During the night she dreamed she and Aaron were standing on El Perico Mesa overlooking the tent rocks. In her dream Aaron did not speak, but reached out to her and pulled her slowly to him. She laid her face against Aaron's chest and smelled the fragrances of musk and bay rum. Slowly, so slowly, Larissa felt herself being drawn into Aaron's body, and she felt the sensation of King Carlos weaving around their ankles.

Larissa awoke early the next morning with the dream still clear in her mind. In fact, it seemed to be haunting her. She quickly dressed and gathered King Carlos's toys and his blanket. She loaded these things into her van along with some heavy cord and a shovel. She went back into the house, called Mimi, and told her what had happened.

"I need to bury him today," Larissa said.

"Where?" Mimi asked.

"I have a special place in mind, a very spiritual place." Larissa did not want to tell Mimi where she planned to take King Carlos.

"Well, then promise me you'll call when you're done. I want to make sure you're okay." Mimi sounded insistent.

"I promise. Good-bye."

Larissa hurried to leave. She finished putting a few more items into the van and placed King Carlos, still wrapped in the towel, on the passenger seat beside her. She laid him where she could see his face, and then she headed her van north out of Los Espíritus to take her precious pet to El Perico Mesa.

As she drove down the lonely highway, she thought about the events of the past few months. She could not put the break-up with Aaron to rest. She kept going over and over what had happened, and she tried to determine what she should have done differently.

When she approached La Zorilla, Larissa decided not to take the time to stop and proceeded on to the turn off. When she arrived at the dirt road, she hoped it would be in good condition. Although the rainy season had just ended, there appeared to have been no rain in the area for quite some time.

Larissa reached over and touched King Carlos on the head and then proceeded up the steep road. When she arrived on the top, she pulled her van off the narrow road and parked it in the shadows of a stand of tall ponderosa pines. She took King Carlos to the back of the van, and opened the door so she could get his toys and blanket.

"I'm so sorry, King Carlos. It's my fault you're dead. Please forgive me. Oh, God! Please forgive me." She spoke to the animal as if he could hear her, and she said the words, "Please forgive me," over and over.

Larissa tightly bound the cat and his toys in his blanket. She took her shovel to the fir tree where she and Aaron had spent a delightful afternoon making love in her sleeping bag. How happy she had been then. She had thought nothing would ever come between Aaron and her again, but she had been wrong. Now, she sadly searched for a place to dig a hole to bury King Carlos.

Finding the dirt somewhat soft beneath one of the low lying branches of the fir tree, she dug a deep hole, and picked up the bundle which shrouded her dead cat. After holding it a few moments to her breast, she placed it carefully down into the grave.

"We are all a part of a cycle, my dear King Carlos. Now you will be eaten by worms which are eaten by birds which, in turn, are eaten by cats." Larissa picked up the shovel and began filling the hole. "This is your time, King Carlos, to contribute to the cycle instead of taking from it."

After Larissa put the last shovel full of dirt on the grave, she packed it down. Then she went back to her van and sat for a while. She struggled against the strong urge to walk to the edge of the mesa, and look down upon the tent rocks. It was above the tent rocks where she had first encountered Aaron Wolf. It was there where he had told her he loved her. She did not know if she could bear seeing the rock formations without Aaron in her life.

Finally, Larissa left the van and walked through the stand of tall pines, not even looking up when she heard the wind moaning through the tops of the trees. She crossed the clearing and stopped at the edge of the mesa and looked out across the valley below her. The leaves of the alders along the river were trembling in the breeze. Larissa's eyes followed the serpentine growth of trees until it disappeared into the misty distance. The mountains to the east and south appeared a mottled blue because the sun had not climbed high enough to wash away the shadows. Immediately below her the whiteness of the tent rocks glistened.

The rocks seemed to be pulling her toward the edge of the mesa. She took a step forward and looked down. How easy it would be to end the pain that now enveloped her. She could jump off the edge of the mesa down into the tent rocks. If she did, perhaps she would die instantly, her body rolling all the way to the bottom. Maybe she would be stopped by one of the rock formations. She wondered whether she would die immediately or lie injured for days before death came. As she stood there, she pondered these possibilities, almost mesmerized by the lure of the tent rocks.

Larissa did not hear the pickup coming up the dirt road. She wasn't looking when it parked beside her van. Neither did she see the man who emerged from the stand of pines and continued walking toward her. She took another step closer to the edge of the mesa. If she had been looking behind her, she would have seen the man abruptly stop and cup his hands and place them on either side of his mouth.

"I love this woman!" the man yelled.

Larissa turned and saw Aaron coming toward her. She took a step backwards.

Aaron stopped about ten feet from her. "Larissa, don't go any farther."

"How did you know I was here?"

"I called Mimi this morning. We've been talking since I left Los Espíritus." He took a few steps toward her. "I've been in Oklahoma—just got here yesterday to take care of some business before

I leave for Alaska." He took several more steps. "Mimi told me about King Carlos and your special spiritual place to bury him. I knew it had to be here." He held his arms out to her. "Come to me, Larissa."

"No! You said you loved me! You beguiled me and then you abandoned me!" She narrowed her eyes and lowered her voice. "What kind of a horrible man are you?"

"Just a man who loves you." He slowly inched forward, closing the gap between them.

"I don't believe anything you say." Larissa shook her head violently.

"I'm sorry, Larissa." Aaron took another step toward her.

She held her hand up as a signal for him to stop, and covered her mouth with the palm of her other hand in an attempt to stop crying.

Neither Aaron nor Larissa moved but stood fixed looking into each other's eyes.

Then Larissa removed her hand from her mouth and screamed, "How could you have believed Epifania Flores?"

Aaron winced. "She played with my mind—like Rubén Silva played with yours." He hesitated for a moment. "I was stupid and I'm profoundly sorry." He reached out for Larissa, but she took a step backwards, and there could be no more steps.

"You said horrible things to me, Aaron. You should have believed me."

Larissa started to turn away from him. However, Aaron grabbed her and pulled her to him. As he tightly held her in his arms, she felt his silver belt buckle dig into her flesh. With her face against his chest she began to sob, her body heaving against his.

He whispered to her, "I'm so sorry, Larissa. I love you. Please believe me. I love you."

They stood for a while with him tightly embracing her. Her spirit began to stir deep within her. Familiar sensations ran up her arms and into her shoulders and down her spine. Her spirit awakened and began searching for his.

"Larissa, let's leave this place. I don't like it here."

The sound of Aaron's voice caused her to open her eyes. She saw he had taken his arms from around her and was now holding her hand. He led her away from the tent rocks and into the pines. They got into their vehicles and started down the mountain just as the sun reached its zenith.

The sun shone down on El Perico Mesa making the tent rocks glisten and shimmer. Along the river, alder leaves fluttered, and the banks along the river appeared to be alive with movement. The green and blue of pine and spruce were easily distinguished on the mountains across the valley. Larissa wasn't aware of any of this because all she saw was Aaron's pickup truck in her rearview mirror.

Chapter Nineteen

During the drive back to Los Espíritus, Larissa reflected on what had just happened. She wondered if Aaron would want her to marry him. The thought of going to Alaska frightened her, and leaving New Mexico might be something she could not do at this time. She had established a strong spiritual bond with the place of her birth, but she still felt a bond with Aaron. Now, she asked herself if she could trust the strength of the love which Aaron and she had professed for one another. Their love for one another had already been shaken, too easily perhaps.

When they arrived at Larissa's house, Aaron went in with her. The house seemed lonely without King Carlos. Aaron did not mention the cat and Larissa was relieved for that. She prepared a light meal and a pot of coffee, and they sat across from one another at the dining room table as they had many times during the past year. They talked very little. Larissa seemed caught up in her own thoughts about how difficult her life would be without Aaron.

Finally, Larissa spoke. "I have news for you. Eloy Flores has been dismissed from the College."

Aaron looked surprised. "Eloy didn't mention this to me when we talked yesterday." Aaron shook his head in apparent disbelief. "Well, did it take a lot of evidence to get rid of him?"

"There were a few depositions, especially from a couple of the female students. This information seemed to go harder against him than all of the nasty things he did to me." Larissa put the lid on the sugar bowl. "And going off and leaving you in the snowstorm didn't seem to be an issue against Eloy at all."

"I'm not surprised. I'm impervious to the elements. Remember?" Aaron drank the last of his coffee.

Larissa continued, "That's not all. Epifania told the investigator that I had made up the entire case against Eloy. She even accused me of luring him to my office, stealing his clothes, and leaving him naked. It's true, the campus security guard found him naked in the museum building. Epifania was chasing Eloy and beating him with a stick she had supposedly found propping the front door open. That was the final blow to Eloy's tenure." Larissa stopped a moment to laugh. "It was a good thing Carmelita swore to the investigator that on the day in question, I was home with an upset stomach. She reported she even had made me a cup of *manzanilla* tea."

Aaron smiled at the mention of one of Carmelita's special teas. "And what did the investigator say about that?"

"He wanted to know if the tea had given me any relief. Carmelita told him of course it did because her remedies always work."

Aaron sat quietly watching Larissa as she folded her napkin. They were silent for a good while.

Finally, Larissa said, "Aaron, I need to know the truth. Do you still believe what Epifania Flores told you about Eloy and me?" Larissa looked down at her plate.

"No, I don't believe it."

Larissa looked up and fixed her eyes intently on Aaron's face. "What made you change your mind?"

"The thought of you and Eloy together didn't make any sense to me. Neither did the ridiculous idea of you having sex in your office. I figured if you were into office sex, then you and I would have participated in it—and we never did." He slowly shook his head. "But the main reason I couldn't continue to believe Epifania's story is Eloy himself. He told me Epifania made up the story to get back at you. He said I'd be a fool to lose you."

Larissa said nothing for several moments, but she did not look away from him.

Finally, she said, "So, are you saying that if Eloy hadn't told you the truth, you may have always believed what that stupid Epifania had told you?" Larissa felt a little anger welling up inside of her.

"No, I can't say that. I've already told you why I had a hard time believing Epifania in the first place. Also, I honestly thought I could trust you. But I have been fooled before by a woman I totally trusted." Aaron stopped, picked up his coffee cup, and then put it back down. "I guess, at first, I thought you had done me the same way."

"But you didn't catch me in the act like you did the other woman!" Larissa stopped short because she thought she should not have said anything about the Oklahoma woman.

"How do you know about that?" Aaron asked.

"When I first met you, Eloy told me about the woman in Oklahoma. He said you didn't trust women because of what she had done to you."

Aaron did not respond.

"Well, I'm not like your woman in Oklahoma. I've been faithful to you, but you called me a whore." Larissa covered her face with her hands and began crying.

"I was very angry. I'm sorry." Aaron reached over and took her hands away from her face.

She pulled her hands away from him. "If I'm a whore, I've been exclusively your whore!"

"Listen, Larissa, I came over here the next morning after I had talked badly to you. I came to tell you I was sorry and had said things I didn't mean, but you weren't here. You were on your way to Albuquerque. I also came the next night, but you wouldn't come to the door." He sat back in his chair. "I'm sorry I believed Epifania. I shouldn't have called you a whore—I shouldn't have said I didn't love you. What more do you want me to say?"

"Aaron, I want you to say you made a mistake and our breakup is entirely your fault. I want to hear you say you understand how much you have hurt me." Her voice broke, and she began to weep.

"I've already told you all of that. Didn't you understand anything I said? That should have been enough for you!" Aaron spoke loudly.

Larissa realized Aaron seemed flustered and apparently angry. Perhaps he thought he had verbalized this, but she did not interpret it as such. Maybe in his mind he had told her what he thought she wanted to hear, but he had not said it to suit her. She wondered how badly he had been hurt by his painful breakup with the woman in Oklahoma. Perhaps he really could not trust a woman again.

Larissa stopped crying and wiped her eyes with her napkin. Then she said, "This school year should be more pleasant at the College, and I feel I can really put my energy and heart into the museum. I need to have the museum completed and open to the public by the end of the spring semester."

Aaron looked down and bit his bottom lip. Then he looked up at Larissa and reached across the table and took her left hand. "Larissa, please, I need you to be with me. Will you marry me and come with me to Alaska?"

She hesitated and then replied, "I don't think I can at this time. I don't know if I ever can." She noticed he seemed to be looking at the turquoise ring which she still wore on her left hand. "Aaron, I won't take it off, but I need to heal my spirit before I can think about marrying you. This has hurt me more than you realize." She stopped and took a deep breath. "Maybe I will go to Alaska later, after I complete my commitments to the College. And there's Rubén Silva's trial. I have to be here for that." She shrugged and looked away from Aaron, "I have to put a lot of things behind me. It's very important to me to do all of that first. Then, and only then, can I marry you."

He tightened his grip on her hand. "Does it make any difference to you knowing how much I love you?"

"It makes no difference, not even knowing how much *I* love you." She pulled her hand away from his. "I wish I didn't love you, it would make saying good-bye much easier."

He took several deep breaths before speaking. "I can see now what I've done to you. I understand why you are in so much pain and I hope you can forgive me. Can't you see I'm also hurting?'

She said nothing. They sat and silently looked at one another for a while.

Finally, he said, "Thank you for supper. I guess I'd better go." He stood up and put his chair back under the table. "I'll call you every Sunday. And if you want to join me in Alaska, I'll be waiting for you."

As she realized he was leaving, she felt a sense of panic. "Aaron, please don't go to Alaska. You don't need a better paying job. You can stay here in Los Espíritus with me. I have enough money for us."

He slowly shook his head and said, "And what else would you do to me, Larissa? Remove my front claws?"

She did not respond. He had made it obvious how he felt about her impulsive suggestion. This came as no surprise to her. She realized she should not have said it.

Larissa walked with Aaron to the front door. As he started to put his hand on the knob, she took his hand and pulled him toward her. Maybe she should say again how much she loved him and would always love him. Perhaps she needed to say she forgave him and desperately wanted to go with him to Alaska. At least, she must let him know how much she would miss him.

"Hold me, Aaron," she whispered.

As they embraced, she laid her cheek against his chest and smelled the faint odor of bay rum. She sensed the beating of his heart and the warmth of his breath on the top of her head, and then she realized he was crying. Suddenly, without warning, she felt her body being drawn into his, and she perceived his spirit indisputably strengthening its hold on her spirit. At that moment, she decided she did not need to tell him anything about her feelings toward him. She was sure he already knew.

Chapter Twenty

The fall semester at the College had begun by the time Rubén Silva's trial came about. Rubén had pleaded not guilty, causing Larissa to have to suffer through the trauma and humiliation of testifying about the acts he had carried out against her. Braulio seemed to welcome the opportunity to tell the jury what he had witnessed the night he had walked into Larissa's bedroom.

"That maniac needs to be put away forever for what he did to Larissa," Braulio had told the jury and anyone else who had mentioned the trial to him and some who had not. "I should have given him several more whacks with my baseball bat. He'd be in his grave now instead of in a courtroom costing us taxpayers a lot of money."

Carmelita attended the trial, and sat on the back row in the courtroom saying her rosary under her breath. To protect herself from evil, she wore a large silver cross around her neck, as well as several cloves of garlic on a string. She insisted Larissa also wear a string of garlic, but Larissa refused. To placate Carmelita, Larissa put a small clove of the stinky stuff inside her bra between her breasts.

Mimi did not miss one minute of Rubén's trial, and she sat on the front row in a new purple frock, outfitted with beautiful accessories. Several times the bailiff had to tell her to keep her bangle bracelets quiet or he would have to confiscate them. Mimi had asked the District Attorney after the trial why Rubén had collected the documents which

Larissa had found in the file folders in the apartment.

The District Attorney answered, "I think Silva had designs on Miss Lozoya and he became obsessive of her. He probably thought she would be a good catch with all of her assets, so he set about attempting to steal her away from Aaron Wolf. But, undoubtedly, things went awry, and she angered him."

Larissa, who heard all of this, said nothing, but she knew the truth. She was well aware Rubén Silva wanted nothing more from her than the money he thought her father had somehow stolen.

Rubén's defense attorney tried to depict Larissa as a loose and promiscuous woman. He suggested Larissa had lured Rubén into her bedroom for a night of wild and kinky sex. Rubén merely did to Larissa the things she had asked him to do, like handcuffing her and cutting her hair with his hunting knife. When Rubén's attorney had finished this scenario, a number of people in the audience booed, and Trixie Trujillo's voice could be heard above all the others.

Trixie surprised Larissa by sending her a note saying how much she despised what Rubén Silva had done and hoped he got put in jail for a hundred years. Trixie even offered to attest in court to any lie about Ruben that Larissa wanted. Larissa thanked her, but turned down her offer.

When Larissa testified, she sat erect and looked occasionally into the face of Rubén Silva. On the surface, she appeared calm and self-assured all during her testimony, although truthfully, she was frightened. The defense attorney attempted to unnerve her, but without success. Larissa told her story and answered questions without wavering. Her testimony seemed believable and effective.

Some of the most interesting testimony against Rubén came from Madeline Wolf who had come from Oklahoma for the trial. She told the jury about the telephone call she had received from Larissa. Then Madeline described to the jury the attack as she had heard it over the telephone. She said she definitely heard Larissa repeatedly call her attacker Rubén and several times she heard Larissa call him Rubén Silva.

Larissa appreciated Madeline's testimony and was happy to see the young woman. During the two days that Madeline stayed at Larissa's house, the two women talked about a lot of things, but mostly about Aaron. Madeline answered a lot of Larissa's questions about Aaron's life. She also talked about her sister Rosa whose husband recently had been released from prison.

As Madeline prepared to leave Los Espíritus, she said to a tearful Larissa, "Don't be sad, my sister. The next time we meet, we shall cry tears of happiness."

It had taken the jury less than an hour to find Rubén Silva guilty. After Rubén received the conviction and sentence, Larissa was determined to put him and his vicious attack behind her forever. Her list of unfinished business was indeed shrinking.

A few days after the trial, the Coors beer deliveryman came into the cantina. He mentioned to

Mimi about Rubén Silva having a history of beating women.

"I knew Rubén Silva in Colorado, and he was bad news, especially for the women. He was married four or five times, and I heard all of them divorced him because of his violence." According to the deliveryman, Rubén had a vile and vicious temper. "Your little friend is probably lucky he didn't kill her. That kind of man usually does end up killing someone."

With her mind free of the trial and the stress it had brought her, Larissa realized how empty her life seemed without Aaron. Fortunately, the additional new duties she had been assigned at the College helped to ease some of the loneliness Aaron's absence brought her. Because the anthropology department did not expect to replace Eloy until the spring semester; Larissa had been assigned to teach two additional classes. With a teaching load of three classes and the continued work in the museum, she found little time for sitting around and sulking.

Pete Ríos seemed very pleased with Larissa's work and her willingness to take on additional duties. On a very chilly morning, he came down to the museum and found Larissa shivering and wrapped in her red shawl.

He stopped in the doorway to her office and said, "Well, it looks like you're ahead of schedule with the dioramas. I'm very happy with what I see here in the museum. And I've gotten lots of good feedback from the students in your classes." Pete

Ríos hesitated, smiled, and then said, "Maybe we won't need to replace Eloy after all."

"Oh, yes we do need to replace him," Larissa quickly replied. "There are a lot of artifacts I need to prepare for display. I must identify and catalogue them before the end of the spring semester, so we can get this museum opened. I can't do that and continue with the work load I have."

Pete laughed. "Don't worry, Larissa, I'm joking. We've already hired a replacement, and he'll be here for the beginning of the spring semester. He's getting on up in age and a little forgetful, but he's an expert in the field. And he probably won't bother you."

Larissa sighed. "Thank goodness. I don't ever want to work with a man like Eloy again. I'm glad he's out of a job."

Pete Ríos shook his head and smiled. "Oh, he's not out of a job. He found a teaching job at a small college in south Texas. And when he messes up there, they'll get rid of him, and he'll go on somewhere else."

At first Larissa thought of asking for the name of the college where Eloy had gone so she could call and warn someone about him. But she had second thoughts, and decided she did not have time for a crusade which would take a lot of her time and effort. It probably would not even be worth it. Besides, she had too much work to do, and she definitely could put Eloy Flores behind her.

Before Pete Ríos left Larissa's office, he said, "I know it feels a little cold in here, but the College is over its budget, and I had to cut costs in my department somewhere. Since you're the only faculty member using this building, I made the decision not to heat it until it gets really cold. Sorry, Larissa."

Later the same day, José García came by Larissa's office to tell her he had joined the Army and expected to be going to Vietnam soon.

"But how can this be, José? Didn't you get a deferment because you're enrolled in college?" José's news surprised Larissa.

"I was going to get drafted anyway because I'm not a student anymore. Without summer employment with the College, I didn't have enough money for school expenses. And I wasn't able to find any other kind of work." He held his hand out to Larissa. "Thank you, Dr. Lozoya, for always being kind to me."

She stood and held José's hand for a moment. "Stay safe, José. You're a good man and I'll miss you."

After José left, Larissa sat down at her desk. She thought of how the investigation of her complaints against Eloy had kept José from working the summer dig site. The idea of José going to Vietnam upset Larissa. She put her head down on her desk and cried.

214

Chapter Twenty-One

With the advent of the spring semester, Larissa began cleaning the artifacts in her father's den and taking them to the museum. The size of the collection which her father had amassed over the years amazed Larissa. The closet in the den, besides being full of baskets and pottery, also contained some boxes of personal items which Larissa had never seen. Larissa began pulling out the contents and throwing away things that appeared to be of little value.

While cleaning the closet, Larissa came across a brown leather travel bag decorated with hand-painted flowers. The paint had faded and the leather had become cracked and hardened. Larissa had never seen this item before. After dusting the bag, she carefully opened it and found it was full of jars and bottles of what seemed to be toiletries. One of the bottles had a label indicating it contained bay rum and glycerin. She took off the cap and smelled its contents. The odor made her catch her breath, and she pulled her nose away from the bottle. Although a little more intense, it reminded her of the scent of Aaron's hair. Larissa shivered as a strange sensation washed over her. She smelled it again, and she tried to remember something, but it would not come.

"Whose bottles are these? Why are they here in the closet?" Larissa called to Carmelita.

Carmelita came into the den from the kitchen, dried her hands on her apron, and reached for the bottle of bay rum and glycerin. "This was your mother's. I always rubbed this on her skin to keep it soft. I haven't seen this bottle since before she died."

Larissa pulled the bag of toiletries out of the closet so Carmelita could see the contents. "What are these?" Larissa asked.

A look of surprise spread across Carmelita's face. "All of those belonged to your mother. I didn't know your father had kept them." The elderly woman reached into the leather bag, took out a jar and looked at it as she slowly turned it in her hands. "They are very old and dusty. Let me clean them."

Larissa carried the bag into the kitchen and put it on the counter top. "Carmelita, I experience a very strange sensation when I smell the contents of this bottle." Larissa picked up the bottle containing the bay rum and glycerin. "When I smelled this same scent on Aaron, I knew I had smelled it before, but I just couldn't remember where."

"Maybe you smelled it on your mother. She was the only one in this house who used it." Carmelita picked up a dusty jar and began wiping it with a cloth.

"My mother died giving me birth. How could I have smelled it on her?" Larissa looked puzzled.

"She didn't die right away. She lived several months after you were born. A complication of your birth killed her. *Pobrecita*, she just wasn't strong and healthy enough to get over it." Carmelita became silent as she continued cleaning the jars and bottles.

Larissa reached out and touched Carmelita's arm. "Did she ever hold me?"

The elderly woman stopped cleaning and looked at Larissa. "Of course, *m'ija*, she held you. She held you every day, and she even put you to her breast and nursed you for as long as she was able."

Larissa smiled, but asked nothing more about her mother. She looked through the jars and bottles. Most of their contents had dried or had evaporated. After Larissa had removed all the bottles from the bag, she noticed a finger hole in the inside bottom of the bag. On further inspection, Larissa realized the bottom seemed closer to the top than it should have been. She stuck her finger into the hole and pulled up a false bottom. There below it lay numerous bundles of money. Larissa gasped and returned the false bottom into its place just as Carmelita turned back toward Larissa.

"I'll keep only this one," Larissa said and held up the bottle of bay rum and glycerin. "Please throw all the rest away." She put her nose to the opened bottle again, but she no longer sensed she had something buried deep in her memory. Instead, she felt a strong desire to put her arms around Aaron Wolf and bury her face in his long hair. Taking the bottle of bay rum and glycerin, along with the leather bag, to her bedroom, Larissa sprinkled a few drops of the bottle's contents on her bed pillow. That night she slept better than she had slept in a long, long time.

* * *

By the time the spring semester at the College had come to an end, José García was dead.

He had been killed in Vietnam, and his body had been sent back to Los Espíritus for burial. Carmelita and Larissa attended the service. José had a military burial with the flag-draped casket and soldiers firing their rifles in salute to the fallen soldier. Carmelita jumped at the loud volleys of shots, and Larissa clenched her teeth and wondered if José had heard the blast which had sent the fatal bullet ripping through his body. She sadly thought of the naïve, young man in the coffin who had never been any farther away from home than Denver. Then the government sent him half-way around the world to be killed fighting in a war which Larissa had not yet come to understand. She wondered if José had understood it.

As she watched the grief displayed by José's mother, Larissa became too angry to shed tears. She felt enraged, not only toward God, but toward the Communists, the Vietnamese, President Lyndon Baines Johnson, and the government of the United States of America. Most of all, she felt anger toward herself because she should have helped José financially, but she did not. Her money could have kept him in college, but being so involved in her own problems, she did not think about aiding José. It would have been so little on her part, and it would have saved his life. Now it was too late. José was gone forever.

After the funeral, Larissa took Carmelita home, and then she headed her van north toward El Perico Mesa. For some reason which she could not fully grasp, she had a strong desire to stand above the tent rocks where she had first encountered

218

Aaron Wolf. She wanted to be in the place where they had stood on the day he had given her the turquoise ring and told the world he loved her. Most of all, she wanted to be alone and ponder what else she needed to put behind her.

Arriving at La Zorilla, Larissa stopped her van in front of Nicanor Gallegos's service station. She rolled down her window glass and gazed in disbelief at the adobe building which had housed Nicanor's business. Part of its roof had collapsed leaving only three walls standing. The above-ground gasoline tank had been removed, but the usual abundance of junk still lay scattered outside the building. Larissa moved the van forward a few feet so she could look out behind the station building. Nicanor's small house appeared dismal and abandoned. It had no glass left in the windows, and the unpainted door hung tenuously on its last hinge. Larissa was bewildered by how much things had changed in less than a year. She sighed and attempted to adjust the radio station but gave up and drove her van back onto the highway.

Half an hour later, she turned onto the desolate dirt road leading up to the top of El Perico Mesa. On top, she stopped among the pines and sat for a few minutes, watching two Stellar jays as they flitted from tree to tree, loudly calling to one other. Then Larissa got out of her van and looked for the fir tree where she had buried King Carlos. She easily found it. Thinking about the death of her cat renewed the feelings of the guilt she harbored about King Carlos's death. She needed to forgive herself, and she needed to heal. Most of all, she needed to put the guilt and anger behind her, but she realized she could not do it alone.

Finally, she walked toward the northwest end of the mesa. As she crossed the clearing, she anticipated the usual excitement of seeing the tent rocks, but when she reached the edge and looked down upon them, she felt nothing. She saw Aaron's village of the tribe of giants, but without Aaron, the rocks seemed to have little appeal. Suddenly, a terrifying feeling of profound loneliness swept over her. She needed Aaron now more than ever.

At last, she fully understood that the rock formations had actually never fascinated her. It had been the man who had stood with her looking down at the tent rocks. It had been he who had instilled in her spirit the strength for which she now was desperately searching. If she did not go to him, she would never know if Carmelita had been correct about their destiny. She would never be sure if the love she and Aaron had professed for one another was real. If she did not go to him, her spirit would never be healed.

Larissa gazed northwest across the wide river valley toward the tall mountains in the distance. Her inner voice loudly said to her, *Larissa, you foolish woman. Why are you still here?*

Quickly, she returned to her van and drove down the dirt road which took her to the highway and back to Los Espíritus. She had put the tent rocks behind her forever.

Chapter Twenty-Two

On the first day of June, the Santa Elena College Museum of Anthropology opened to the public. Pete Ríos appeared to be ecstatic with the excellent reviews and kudos he was receiving from the public. In addition, the faculty, the dean, the president of the College, and the members of the Board of Regents all lauded Pete Ríos for the wonderful work he had accomplished in three years.

Of course, Pete Ríos said to some people, "I shouldn't take all the credit. Larissa Lozoya also contributed to this achievement." Sometimes, however, Pete Ríos completely forgot to mention Larissa at all.

The local newspaper ran a front-page article about the new museum along with a photo. The three men shown in the photo congratulating Pete Ríos were, as expected, the College's dean, its president, and the chairman of its Board of Regents. Apparently no one remembered to contact Larissa so she could be included in the photo. That same evening, she busied herself at home, going through her clothing and personal possessions deciding what she wanted to keep and what she wanted to give to the Salvation Army.

* * *

By the time the College summer session had begun, Larissa had totally cleaned out her father's den, as well as all of the closets and drawers in every room in the house. Carmelita seemed surprised by the amount of cleaning Larissa had accomplished. Larissa worked late into the nights, cleaning and packing and organizing her household goods. Carmelita probably did not realize Larissa had been sleeping only four to five hours every night. Most nights Larissa slept in the living room on the sofa, not even bothering to put on her pajamas.

One Saturday morning, Carmelita walked into the living room and, with a loud shriek, apparently awakened the soundly sleeping Larissa.

"What's wrong?" Larissa slowly sat up.

"*El oso*, he's gone! Where is he? What have you done with the bear?" Carmelita stood in the middle of the living room looking down at the place where Brother Bear once had lain.

Larissa looked at Carmelita with half-opened eyes. "I rolled him up and put him in a box."

"Why did you do that?" Carmelita put her hands on her hips and glared at Larissa.

"Because you need to shampoo this ugly, horrible, dirty carpet. Just look at it!" Larissa pointed to a configuration of a bear-skin rug on the carpet.

It had been created because the part of the carpet which had been exposed over the years had faded. Underneath Brother Bear, the carpet had retained its original bright ruby red color.

"*Válgame Dios*, I don't know how to shampoo carpets. Why don't you just buy a new carpet?" Carmelita turned around and went back to the kitchen.

"That's a good idea," said Larissa, and she jumped up from the sofa and walked over to a corner in the living room and pulled back the carpet. She stopped and stared down at the floor. "Come look at this, Carmelita. There are beautiful ceramic tiles under this ugly wool carpet." Larissa pulled back more carpet.

"I don't need to come and look at ceramic tiles," Carmelita called from the kitchen. "I remember the floor. Your father covered the tiles with the carpet when you were learning to walk, so you wouldn't hurt yourself when you fell."

Later the same day, Carmelita watched from the window as Larissa instructed two men to carry several large boxes from the front porch out to a freight delivery truck. One of the boxes was long and narrow. Carmelita saw the men take the boxes away. Being suspicious, Carmelita roamed the house all afternoon trying to determine what Larissa could have possibly sent away in the boxes. While Carmelita took mental inventory of the household goods, Larissa disposed of the living room carpet. By evening, she had swept, mopped, and polished the tile floor. She called Carmelita into the living room to inspect the job.

"It looks nice, *m'ija*. Now you can put *el oso* back on the floor." Carmelita stood surveying the ceramic tiles. "Let me help you put him back in his place."

"He's not here, my dear Carmelita." Larissa was lying on her back on the sofa looking up at the ceiling.

"*Ay, Dios mío*." Carmelita shook her finger at Larissa. "You've thrown away so many things lately, and you've given things away. You haven't donated your father's bear to someone, have you?"

"Oh, no, I sent him on a trip." Larissa smiled and continued looking at the ceiling.

"Where did you send him?" Carmelita asked and raised her left eyebrow extremely high.

"I sent him north," Larissa said.

Carmelita gasped. "Are you sure he wanted to go?"

"Yes, I am sure, and he will be waiting for me to join him."

Chapter Twenty-Three

Mimi's bangle bracelets jingled as she drove her Buick Roadmaster at seventy miles an hour down a narrow two-lane highway. With all four windows open, the wind whipped her long, red hair in all directions about her head, and she occasionally brushed her hair from in front of her eyes. On this warm July day, Mimi, Larissa, and Carmelita were approaching Albuquerque in an automobile with no air conditioning.

"What did Pete Ríos say when you told him you were resigning?" Mimi looked at Larissa who sat in the front-passenger seat.

"He told me I'd better think twice because I might never get another job as good as the one I had at Santa Elena." Larissa stifled a giggle and rolled her eyes. She was pleased with how easily she had put Santa Elena College behind her.

"Pete Ríos is an arrogant ass," Mimi said.

Carmelita, sitting in the back seat with her eyes tightly closed and her rosary in her hand, smiled. Then she returned to weeping. She had been crying off and on ever since they had left Los Espíritus earlier in the morning.

Larissa looked over at Mimi. "You can slow down. We aren't going to be late for goodness sakes. You're scaring Carmelita."

"For the love of God, please tell me what Carmelita isn't scared of?" Mimi slowed her automobile's speed just a little.

Larissa tried to keep her own hair from flying around but, with the windows open, she

225

found it impossible. "And why don't you buy a new car, Mimi, one with air conditioning? I know you can afford it."

"I don't need a new car. Where do I go? I don't go anywhere that I should need a new car." Mimi chuckled. "Besides, I can use your van whenever I want." Mimi slowed down as they entered the city limits of Albuquerque. "And Braulio sure seemed happy when you gave it to him."

Larissa rolled up the window glass on her side and began brushing her hair. "Yes, I know it made Braulio happy. And, just think, he will have a nice air-conditioned vehicle, and you'll still have this old clunker."

"This old clunker has taken you many places. And you, too, Carmelita." Mimi patted the discolored and crackled dashboard as her bracelets jangled loudly.

Larissa quickly turned in the seat and faced Mimi. "Did I tell you that Pete Ríos told me Eloy got a job teaching at a college in south Texas? I can't believe men like him get away with what they do."

Mimi laughed and said, "And did I tell you Epifania refused to go with him?" Mimi slowed the automobile as they entered a busy boulevard. "Their neighbor told me all about it one day when he came into the cantina."

Carmelita slapped the back of Mimi's seat." You have that wrong. *La cabrona* didn't refuse to go, *el cabrón* refused to take her with him. And I know that's the truth because Epifania's maid told me, and she's not one for idle gossip." Then Carmelita leaned forward, reached over the seat, and patted Larissa on the cheek. "*Ay, m'ija*, how can I live without you?"

"My dear, Carmelita, it's not like I'm dying. I'll be home from time to time. Just take care of my house for me." Larissa looked back and smiled at the elderly woman.

Mimi turned the Buick onto a street leading to the airport. "Larissa, do you want me to park in the parking lot, so we can go into the terminal building with you?"

"No. It will be too hard on Carmelita. By the time I get inside and get my baggage checked, it will be almost time to board my plane. Just pull up into the unloading zone, and I'll get a skycap to help me take my things in."

Mimi parked the Buick alongside the curb, and the three women got out. Mimi opened the trunk and a skycap arrived to get Larissa's luggage. As he reached for the brown leather bag decorated with painted flowers, Larissa quickly picked it up and told the man she would take it. Carmelita blessed Larissa several times and made the sign of the cross with her gnarled hand. Larissa thanked Carmelita for her blessings and reached into the back seat and pulled out a pet carrier. She kissed each of the women and told them she loved them. Carmelita blessed her one more time and then kissed Larissa on both cheeks.

As Larissa walked away with the brown leather bag in one hand and the pet carrier in the other, she did not try to fight back the tears that were streaming down her face. She knew these women were a part of her life that she could never put behind her. Forcing a smile to her lips, she looked back at them, then turned and walked into the terminal.

Larissa arrived at the ticket desk just behind the skycap who gave her baggage to the agent to tag. After setting the pet carrier down on the floor and the leather bag between her feet, she handed some papers and her ticket to the agent.

The agent looked at the ticket. "One way to Anchorage, Alaska. Right?"

"Yes." Larissa answered and bent over and picked up the pet carrier. She raised the carrier to eye level and looked in at her yellow cat. "Now, my dear King Carlos, we are going to be separated for a while, and if you're a real good cat today, I'll give you a whole can of tuna fish when we arrive in Anchorage." She handed the pet carrier to the agent, picked up the brown leather bag, and headed for the boarding gate with a big smile on her face.

After boarding, Larissa sat down in her seat by a window and placed the leather bag snugly under her seat. Then, she fastened the seat belt loosely around her body, closed her eyes, and tried to relax. She thought about where she and King Carlos the Tenth would be in just a matter of hours, and then she smiled to herself.

The attendants gave their safety spiel about seat belts and exit doors, but Larissa did not pay any attention. She had already heard all of this during the years she had flown back and forth from boarding school. Right now, she just wanted to relax and maybe sleep. Sleeping would help make the time go by faster. Most of all, she needed to calm herself because she felt a trembling inside of her body. The airplane rushed down the runway and, as it lifted, a feeling of exhilaration swept through Larissa. The airplane banked and then headed northwest. Larissa closed her eyes and let her body relax.

If Larissa had been looking out the windows of the airplane, she would have seen the juniper covered mesas below and the higher mountains to the north and east. If she had looked carefully, she may have seen stands of ponderosa pines in the distance. More than likely she would have noted when the cottonwoods along the river were replaced with alders. But Larissa did not see any of this. She had tightened her seatbelt and had placed her hand on its buckle. She was thinking of another buckle, a silver one set with turquoise stones. With her eyes closed, she envisioned the man who wore this buckle. He also wore jeans, a western shirt, and a wide-brimmed hat. He would be waiting for her and her cat at the Anchorage airport.